I0587114

SNAKE HANDLIN' MAN

ROCK BAND FIGHTS EVIL #2

SNAKE HANDLIN' MAN

ROCK BAND FIGHTS EVIL #2

D.J. Butler

 **WordFire Press**
Colorado Springs, Colorado

SNAKE HANDLIN' MAN
Copyright © 2012 D.J. Butler

ISBN: 978-1-61475-301-8

Cover painting by Carter Reid

Cover design by Janet McDonald

Art Director Kevin J. Anderson

Book Design by RuneWright, LLC
www.RuneWright.com

Published by
WordFire Press, an imprint of
WordFire, Inc.
PO Box 1840
Monument CO 80132

Kevin J. Anderson & Rebecca Moesta, Publishers

WordFire Press Trade Paperback Edition April 2015
Printed in the USA
wordfirepress.com

CHAPTER ONE

I assume none of you guys has anything against strippers?"

Owen had the dusky olive skin and dark hair that said he was a classic American mutt, some Eastern Europe in him, maybe Serb or Greek, some Latin America, some who-knew-what. He was a heavy man, not in the *this-guy-eats-Twinkies-for-breakfast* way, but in the *this-guy-can-wrestle-a-Peterbilt-to-the-asphalt* way. Also, Eddie had noticed as the man waved at them coming in through the door of the diner, he was packing. It was a big pistol, not particularly hidden in a shoulder holster under Owen's slightly shabby sport coat.

Eddie respected that. He had his Glock in a shoulder holster, too. When the rubber hit the road, of course, he preferred his Remington 870 Express Magnum, a twelve-gauge pump action with its stock shortened and its barrel cut down. He had other guns, other shotguns, even, but the 870 was his favorite. A single slug from the 870 was enough for any human attacker, and most minor minions of Hell. But you couldn't just walk into a diner with a sawed-off shotgun and ask for coffee.

Not even in Oklahoma.

"We ain't proud," Eddie grunted.

"Good," Owen pounded the Formica table with one meaty fist. "It's a small stage, and you're gonna to have to share."

"They have boobs, right?" Mike asked. The big bass player grinned like he was kidding. He was jumpy, but he'd handled himself well in New Mexico, and Eddie didn't mind having him along, even if Jim did see the Left Hand on the guy. For that matter, the fact that he was on Heaven's bad side made him fit in better with the band.

"Mike's no homophobe," Adrian sneered. "Women or trannies, either way. Beggars can't ... well, you know what they say about beggars."

Owen roared with laughter and pounded the table again. Behind the club manager, Eddie saw a sheet of flame. Men hung in it like worms baiting fish, the tips of enormous hooks protruding through their chests. Their feet twitched, gore ran down their bellies and legs, their mouths worked the shapes of tormented howling, but Eddie heard nothing.

He could see Hell, thank Heaven he didn't have to hear it. He rubbed his eyes with the palms of his hands while the vision faded. He'd needed the money, he reminded himself. He'd sold his soul because he wanted to be a good man and wanted his kids to eat bread that wasn't marked down because it was stale for once. The visions didn't come from him, didn't reflect him—they were his punishment for one really stupid choice.

He'd screwed it up six ways to Sunday, but he'd meant to do it for Sharon and the girls.

"This ain't that kind of town," Owen chuckled, "and Correia's ain't that kind of joint. But I got a tip on a place in Amarillo, if that's what you're into. Never been there myself, you understand, but I'm an open-minded guy."

"Jeez," Mike grumbled, elbowing Adrian in the ribs.

"What'll you have?"

The waitress was clean and pretty. She had the look of a self-improver about her, her uniform clean even though it was a horrible orange and brown polyester, her flat shoes shined and spotless even though she'd obviously bought them at PayLess, her hair back in a neat ponytail. Also, she wasn't chewing gum, which was a plus. And she was very pregnant. The plastic rectangle pinned to her chest read *SAMANTHA*.

"Coffee," Eddie said instantly. "Don't bother making a fresh pot."

2

"In fact," Twitch said, his eyes sparkling across the corner booth, "if you can use water from the urinal, Eddie would prefer it. He likes his punishment self-inflicted."

Eddie harrumphed, ignoring the jab from the fairy drummer. "Chicken-fried steak and gravy for the big guy," he added, jerking his thumb at Jim. Jim nodded quietly and smiled, big pale goth-looking son of a bitch that he was. Big but thin, no matter what he ate. Probably got that indestructible physique from his father, who was Azazel himself, head of the Infernal Council and Prince of Darkness. "And a large Pepsi."

"Ooh," she said, making a tight circle of her lips and exhaling sharply. She rubbed her own belly and then grinned. "He's kicking." She wrote down Jim's lunch.

"Pie, Samantha," Mike jumped in. "A slice of your best. No, one slice each of your two best."

"That would be coconut cream," she said, "and coconut cream. She leaned in close to the bass player, her breasts brushing his shoulder. "The rest of it is Alpo."

"Thanks." Mike laughed.

She nodded and noted the pie on her pad. "You can call me Sami."

"Are your eggs from free range chickens?" Adrian asked.

"Nope," Sami said. "They're from the Costco in Guymon."

Adrian sighed and shook his head. The wizard was finicky. He seemed to think his new age lifestyle was a necessary component of his sorcery; Eddie doubted it but didn't care. The patchouli oil and the incense and the morning exercise routine didn't get in the rest of the band's way, any more than Eddie's visions did.

"Don't fret about it," Eddie told him. "You do enough yoga for you and the chickens both."

"Besides," Mike got in a lick, "free range eggs aren't going to be enough to keep you awake."

"I'll take two eggs anyway," Adrian shrugged, glaring at the bass player. "Scrambled. No toast, unless you have whole wheat without high fructose corn syrup."

"Mmmm," purred Sami, the waitress, in a friendly way, "a man who takes care of himself." Her accent was pleasant and twangy, more deep Texas than Oklahoma, it seemed to Eddie.

"This body is a high performance instrument," Adrian sniffed, "called upon frequently to perform extraordinary feats. You drive a Formula One car, you can't just pull into the Chevron and fill the tank with Unleaded."

"In fact," Twitch said, "if you drive a Formula One car, it turns out that you mostly leave it in the garage. Scrambled eggs for me, too, darling, and I'll have the toast, as long as it's made out of bread."

"Two eggs," Sami noted, "one toast." She frowned a sad frown at Adrian and patted him on the shoulder. She wasn't wearing a wedding ring, Eddie couldn't help noticing. "And for you, Owen?" she asked.

Owen shook his head. "I got a sack lunch in the desk," he said. "You know me."

Sami smiled at all of them. "I'll be right back," she promised. As she turned to go, Eddie got a good look at her swollen belly. She was just about ready to pop, he realized. He remembered when Sharon had looked like that, in the last days of each of her pregnancies. He shut out the memories, concentrated on the table.

"Cash," he said to Owen. "Cash is the important thing."

"I remember," Owen nodded. "No worries."

"Your accountant okay with it? We don't exactly do our taxes."

"I am the accountant," the big man said. "And I'm okay with it. Most of our local traffic pays in cash, so it'll be easy to fix."

"That's what I like to hear."

"I don't get you," Mike said to Eddie, gulping his ice water. One sip of the water had been enough for Eddie; it tasted like sand and chlorine.

"Yeah?" Eddie looked around the diner, staying alert. Cracked linoleum, peeling faux-wood, dirty glass. Ageing donuts and cookies in a bell-shaped glass display next to the khaki-colored cash register, vintage 1980 or older. Posters of Elvis and Marilyn Monroe and James Dean peeling away from Scotch tape faded into yellow visibility. A truck driver scarfing down a foot long sandwich in one corner and two old women yammering over coffee and biscuits. Or maybe it was black tea. And a big wheel, silver-gleaming, on which the bodies of four young women were impaled and spinning. No one else but Eddie saw this last, of course. "What's not to get?"

Mike looked thoughtfully at Owen, which was good. At least the new guy was conscious enough of what he was saying to be careful around outsiders. "I mean, you live so careful, Eddie."

"Yeah?"

"Yeah. If I was you, I'd try the pie. Mierda, if I was you, I'd eat nothing *but* pie. Pie and donuts."

Mike meant: *if I knew exactly when and how I was going to die, Eddie, like you do, I'd go crazy and stuff myself with pie because it wouldn't matter.*

Well, not *exactly* when and how.

"You'd go crazy with the women, too," Eddie predicted.

"Or the trannies," Adrian threw in.

"Hey," Mike objected.

"Probably skydive and mainline heroin and do anything else, right?" Eddie asked. "Smoke like a chimney, drink like a fish. Because you wouldn't give a damn about the consequences."

Mike nodded.

"So what you're saying," Eddie ground out the logical conclusion of Mike's line of thought carefully, "is that if you were me, you'd give up." He realized that he was inadvertently clenching both his fists, and he made a conscious effort to relax them.

"Uh ..." Mike struggled.

Owen scratched his head. "I think he's just saying live a little, man," the club manager suggested. "I mean, coffee? You gotta have more than coffee."

"I do live a little," Eddie said. "Sometimes I add cream."

"You're a wild man," Owen laughed. "Tonight, I'll run your tab at cost. And the first beer's on Correia's."

Crash!

"Help!" the voice was Sami the waitress's.

Eddie jumped out of his seat and Owen jumped with him, shoulder to shoulder as they both whipped out guns. Behind him, Eddie heard the rest of the band struggling with the confines of the circular table and the corner booth. Twitch could become a falcon at will, but he wouldn't want to do it with this many witnesses. Not unless it was really necessary.

"It's okay!" the cook called. He was scrambling out from the kitchen to the area behind the counter, waving at the diner's customers. "She's okay, she just slipped!"

Eddie noticed Owen's gun. "Desert Eagle," he said admiringly. "Fifty caliber?"

"Made by bad-ass Hebrews," Owen agreed. He nodded at Eddie's pistol. "Glock 18? Selective fire?"

Eddie grinned. "Sometimes you just gotta shoot automatic."

"Hey," Owen shrugged. "You can't always choose when you're gonna have multiple assailants. I respect an informed decision."

"I respect a man whose gun can punch holes through brick walls."

"Aw," Twitch sighed. "They're in love."

"Sami?" the cook yelped. He was a burly man in jeans and a greasy white t-shirt, with no hair to speak of on his head and arms covered in burn scars. He stood up and backed away from the spot behind the counter where the waitress must be lying.

"Aaaaaaagh!" she screamed.

"Jeez!" Mike grabbed the bird's nest of superstitious junk that hung from his neck. Eddie holstered his gun and ran for the counter.

He vaulted over the counter as the cook turned and ran, filling the space the man vacated. Sami lay sprawled against a big plastic bag full of Styrofoam cups, legs akimbo and knees up. Her brown and orange skirt was dark and wet, and Eddie's sadly experienced brain instantly identified the cause.

Samantha sat in a puddle of her own blood.

"Aaagh!" she screamed again, throwing her head back and bucking her hips.

"Easy, girl," Eddie tried to calm her. He'd delivered his own first child, on a midwinter Chicago night when the air was frozen so solid the hospital couldn't force its ambulances out the door, at least not when the call came from Eddie's shitty South Side row of tenements. His own car had been broken down, as always, brakes totally shot. He'd never had a car worth owning. He didn't want to deliver the waitress's kid, but he wasn't about to leave her to her own devices, either.

"My baby!" she shouted at him. Her face was red and straining, the cords of her neck muscles standing out like rope.

"Owen!" Eddie hollered. The old ladies had looked up from their biscuits at the commotion. The trucker was staring, too, mayonnaise and barbecue sauce dripping from all his fingers and staining his flannel shirt. "Who delivers babies in this town?"

"Doc Jensen!" Owen snapped, and dug into his pocket for a cell phone.

"Tell him it's the bottom of the ninth!" If there was already blood, Sami wasn't going anywhere to have her baby.

"Aaagh!"

Eddie turned back to the girl.

"You're going to be okay," he promised her. He tried to ignore the river of fire he saw drifting lazily beneath her hips and the skeletal hands that seemed to be reaching up from within it. "Just hold my hand and tell me where it hurts. Focus on breathing." He felt like an idiot. He hadn't been able to do much for his wife when she'd delivered, either, just held her hand and took her abuse and then caught the baby and toweled it off.

"Aaaagh!" Sami screamed again, twisting her neck like she was riding a bucking bronco, and clawing a handful of Styrofoam from the pile she lay on.

"It's okay—"

A snake stuck its head out from under her skirt. A really big snake.

"What the hell?"

Eddie stumbled back, falling onto his own butt. As he did, a flash of movement in the corner of his eye caught his attention.

Eddie had been freestyle fighting champion of his company in Iraq, unofficial but also uncontested. He had lost muscle since then, but his sinews, nerves and reflexes were as good as they'd ever been. He kicked himself back, slamming upward with the blade of his right hand, deflecting the missile darting in to strike his neck—

his blow connected with a heavy *thwack*—

he knocked the missile straight up into the air over his head, where he got a good look at the thing that was attacking him. It was another snake, this one more normal in size, maybe four or five feet long, red and green and vicious.

Only the snake had wings. Leathery bat's wings, and its wingspan was almost as long as the snake's body.

Hissss!

Then something grabbed his feet. Eddie looked down and saw thick, scaly knuckles tightening their grip on the ankles of each of his combat boots. They dragged forward the thing that emerged from underneath Sami the waitress's skirt, tongue slithering in and out of its diamond-shaped head.

It wasn't a snake. It was a Komodo dragon, or something so similar that Eddie couldn't tell the difference. When it cracked its jaws Eddie saw teeth like shards of glass.

"Jim!" Eddie yelled. "Adrian!"

Another snake popped out from under the waitress's skirt, another flyer that launched itself into the air. She shrieked, a high-pitched, wordless sound of pain that was more like the squeal of a deflating balloon than a noise a human would ever normally make.

Eddie scissor-kicked his boots together, thumping them into the lizard's head behind its jaw, where he hoped the tissues would be soft. His boots were steel-toed and he kicked as hard as he could, but the kick only freed one of his feet, and then the Komodo dragon snapped its mouth at him in rage.

He managed to yank free his pistol as a third flyer popped from underneath Sami's skirt. He felt sick, guessing what was going on under there. She squealed and shuddered like an epileptic. Poor kid.

"Adrian!" he yelled, and pointed the Glock—

bang!—

and shot Sami right between the eyes. Her head snapped back in a flower of bright red blood and then she collapsed, still.

Then the Komodo dragon was on top of him, and Eddie struggled to get an elbow up in front of his face. The thick cloth of his old green jacket saved him from a scratch of the beast's teeth, and then he forced the open mouth away from his face, pinning the jaws between his forearm and the counter's support column under the cash register.

He could still smell the reek of the thing's breath. It stank of sewage.

Eddie heard gunshots as the rest of the band, out of his vision, got into the fight.

"Chingón!" That would be Mike.

The lizard's hind claws scratched at Eddie's hips and pelvis, and again his jacket protected him. Eddie jammed a hand down decisively and grabbed one of the creature's knees. He rolled himself backward, yanking the thing with him—

and hurling it down along the space behind the counter—

crash!—

to where it slammed home against a stack of soda syrup canisters. Like bowling pins, they tumbled around the reptile and rolled in all directions.

Eddie jumped to his feet and thumbed the Glock's selective fire switch to *automatic*. The old ladies screamed and slapped at a snake with handbags. The truck driver clutched at his throat, staining his blond beard with the sauces on his fingers. A snake had bitten him, and the man's face was already turning purple.

Eddie had no time for the dead trucker, but the sight strengthened his resolve not to get bitten himself. He stepped towards the lizard, ducking as he realized that the swarm of winged snakes was thicker than he'd thought, and opened fire.

B-rapp-p-p-p-p-p-p-p!

He squeezed off the entire clip into the canisters and the thrashing body of the lizard. Whatever it was, if bullets could kill it, it was now dead.

The air was full of flying snakes. Adrian chanted something and struggled not to swoon; Jim slammed a pitcher down onto a Formica table top, trapping a serpent under it; Mike swung his M1911 pistol, the one he'd taken off the dead bouncer in New Mexico, looking for a target that would hold still; Owen, the club manager, blasted away at flying snakes with his hand cannon, wearing an expression on his face that might have been *contentment*; Eddie didn't see Twitch. Another winged viper darted at Eddie's head, and he batted it aside with the Glock.

"Oil!" he shouted. The cook peeped out through the order window, wide-eyed and open-mouth. Eddie pointed at him, careful to point with his empty hand and not his pistol. "Oil!" he yelled again. "Now!"

Hissss! he heard behind him, and turned to see more snakes slipping from Sami's skirt. He caught a glimpse of what was behind, and shuddered in sympathetic pain—there was a writhing mass of snakes, and a river of blood.

Eddie heard the pounding of feet and the slamming open of a door. He looked into the kitchen and saw a back door swinging slowly shut, the cook gone.

"Damn!" Eddie raced for the kitchen, slamming the second clip into his Glock and thumbing the fire switch back to *semi-automatic*. As he passed the big lizard on the floor, the one he'd filled with lead, it stirred, slightly. Eddie cursed through his teeth.

A winged serpent whipped out of the kitchen heading for Mike's neck, too fast for him, and he knew he was a goner—

but then a silver wing flashed in his vision and a falcon torpedoed past him—

snatching the serpent from the air with both its claws and crushing its skull with its powerful beak. A long silvery horse's tail snapped behind the falcon like a pennant.

Twitch.

Another serpent hummed in through the order window as Eddie stepped into the kitchen and spotted what he needed—the frying vat, and, under it, a spare jug of oil, like a gas can. The snake attacked, but Eddie saw this one coming, and was ready for it.

He stepped aside, grabbed the snake by the tail and flung it into the hot oil.

Sizzle! A frying meat smell filled the air. Eddie grabbed the handle of a fry basket and jammed it down on top of the winged snake, forcing it deeper into the fry oil in its writhing protest.

"Six piece Quetzalcoatl nuggets," he muttered, "coming right up." He grabbed the handle of the jug, a white plastic five-gallon container, in his left hand, and turned Glock-first back to the fray.

The lizard crouched in the kitchen door, staring at Eddie with beady black eyes. It bled from multiple bullet wounds in its body, but it was moving and it looked pissed.

Beyond, in the chaos of the diner, he saw Adrian drop to the ground. And then the wizard's fallen body was swarmed by flying serpents.

CHAPTER TWO

Eddie threw the oil jug.

He overestimated his own strength, by quite a lot. The jug thudded to a dull halt halfway between him and the lizard, and then the lizard rushed him.

He got the Glock up and into play, squeezing off several rounds and putting at least one of them into the thing before it reached him in an avalanche of claws and teeth. He hurled himself sideways, grabbing for a big squeegee on a pole and jamming it between his own body and the reptile, fending the beast off like a caveman with a sharpened stick. Stab, retreat, stab, retreat, catching the creature on the end of the pole and trying to push it further away. The squeegee's rubber strip tore into shreds under the lizard's assault, leaving a dull tip at the end of the hard pole.

Eddie jumped back to avoid a snap of the jaws that got past his stick. He felt a sudden burning sensation on his own backside, and realized the lizard had forced him so far in reverse that he was sitting on the edge of the grill.

"Damn it!" he shouted, and shoved back on his stick. He got his shoulder into it, scooped the lizard backwards several feet, and then he switched into a staff-fighting stance. He spun the hard wood in an arc that lodged one end of it firmly in the crook of his elbow, and with the other end he battered the lizard in the face with a quick succession of blows.

The creature pulled back, spitting with rage.

Having bought himself a little space, Eddie raised his pistol, aiming the Glock a little higher—

bang!—

and shot a hole in the jug of oil.

Glug, glug, glug, the contents slurped out, filling the kitchen even more with the cloying, dull smell of vegetable oil.

The lizard pushed forward and Eddie jammed the squeegee pole into its face. The beast kept pushing, Eddie shoved back with a fierce snarl, and the makeshift spear snapped in two. Eddie staggered forward and so did the monster and suddenly the big lizard was in his lap, clawing at him and snapping with a mouth like a blender set to *liquefy.*

Eddie jumped back. He fell onto the grill, smelling the scorch-stink of his jacket and feeling the heat intensely, especially on his already burned and stinging buttocks. Above him, gray-white feet hung flaccidly dripping blood, a dozen corpses dangling, each with its neck drilled through by a saber-like tooth in the mouth of a grinning scab-faced fiend. Eddie heard the gunshots and shouting and the zipping of winged serpents through the air behind him like a soundtrack to the infernal carnage he saw overhead. The stink of winged serpent flesh frying past the point of edibility filled his mouth and nose.

He shuddered and kicked.

He caught the lizard square in the center of its face with both his boots and threw it back into the puddle of oil. It hit hard and slipped back, sliding across cracked and mildewed tile in a puddle of canola. Eddie rolled back on his feet, backside and elbows burned and the back of his neck too warm for comfort, but he still held his pistol in his hand and reptilian death in his heart.

The lizard thrashed to regain its footing and scrabbled to try to launch itself at Eddie, jaws gaping. Its maw opened and closed loudly, teeth champing against each other and groping for Eddie's flesh with visible hunger. Eddie didn't waste time shooting it again.

He shot a hole in the fryer, and as the hot oil sloshed out and into the mess on the floor, he kept firing at the metal of the vat.

Bang, bang, bang—

and on the third shot, he got a spark and the hot oil ignited. A sheet of flame like a grassfire sprang into being, rushing across the floor in all directions, and heat and light exploded up at the ceiling in the fryer. The lizard squealed and paddled backward as the fire overtook it, hissing with pain and rage.

Eddie jumped out of the way too, planting one hand in a tub of shredded iceberg lettuce and vaulting up onto his feet on the grill. He could feel the heat of the cooking surface, but the vulcanized rubber soles of his boots kept him from being burned. For the moment.

Eddie had never owned a decent car, but he'd never let himself be without a good jacket and boots. If only he had had a sheet of vulcanized rubber in the seat of his pants, he thought, he wouldn't be feeling the sting of the grill now. He knew Chuck Norris sold rubber-crotch jeans for karate enthusiasts; maybe he sold fireproof-seat pants, too. Really, everyone in the band could probably use a pair.

His speculation was interrupted by a flying serpent whizzing in through the order window. Eddie grabbed it with his left hand, feeling scratchy, shuddering wings inside his clenched fist as he swung the thing around—

and brought it down hard, impaling its head on the order spike. It wasn't much in the way of justice, but it cheered him up a bit to see one of the serpents twitching out its last snake breaths over Mike's double order of coconut cream pie.

Across the kitchen, the burning lizard flailed into a tall set of shelves. They swung forward and crashed to the floor like a hammer, dropping paper-wrapped stacks of paper towels and stacks of toilet paper and cardboard boxes full of paper napkins hurtling through the oil-fire and across the room into its corners. A pile of rags under a big metal double sink burst into flames. Jugs of cleaning chemicals bubbled and tipped over, and thick smoke started to fill the top half of the room.

Heat seared Eddie's lungs. He crouched and jumped, throwing himself headfirst through the order window, tumbling down full-length onto a narrow table behind the counter. He hit the diner's two coffee machines and bounced, all the breath knocked out of him and his body hurting. He struck the floor at the same moment as one of the coffee pots and it shattered, spraying him with hot black coffee.

With his luck, he thought, the one that hadn't shattered was probably the decaf.

Eddie groaned and dragged himself up onto his elbows, patting the puddle of hot coffee to find his pistol again. When he managed to get his eyes opened, he found himself looking at the ruined body of the poor waitress, Sami.

Flying serpents whizzed and hummed about her in a cloud, gnawing the flesh off her body. He fought back a vomit reflex. Probably nothing in his stomach but coffee grounds, anyway.

"Damn snakes!" Eddie jumped to his feet, feeling the heat of the blazing kitchen on his head as he did. He realized that he had shards of coffeepot in his hands and face, but he had no time for that. He grabbed the surviving pot—it was the regular, after all—and tossed its hot contents on the feeding monsters.

They hissed in anger and rose from their interrupted meal, spinning like hummingbirds to face Eddie. And then he heard the teeth-clacking hiss of the bigger reptile behind him, and smelled the stink of oil-charred serpent.

"Ah, nuts," he muttered. "I thought you were dead."

Before and behind him, the waitress's deadly reptilian brood lunged at Eddie.

He dove over the counter, shattering the glass bell full of donuts and cookies with his boots and heading for the floor shoulder-first, trying to come up in a roll.

He hit the tiles next to jeans and boots that he recognized as Jim's. The big man jumped over Eddie as Eddie rolled, and looking up, Eddie saw Jim swinging one of the diner's trays like a club, smacking aside two of the winged snakes with a lunge right, slamming a third onto the countertop with his backswing, and then spinning like a gymnast on a pommel horse to squash another with the back of his boot.

Jim was a swordsman, really. And of course he didn't wear his sword into small town diners, any more than Eddie carried his shotgun. But he was a crazy Cyrano de Bergerac sort of swordsman, as much an athlete and an acrobat as a guy that stabbed with a pointy stick, and he took the battle to the snakes with gusto.

Eddie bumped into Adrian on the floor and stopped his roll. Adrian was turning purple in the face, the livid purple bordered with streaks of yellow that marked an ugly bruise in the height of its flowering. He gasped for air, and he locked his bloodshot, bulging eyes on Eddie's own and choked out a few words.

"Three hours," Adrian managed, and then, "*per Hypnum dormito.*" His body went limp and his head fell back, cracking on the tile.

"Adrian!" Eddie shouted, and pressed his finger against the wizard's neck. Adrian, who was also the band's organ player, often fell asleep in the middle of trying to cast a spell—he was cursed—but he didn't usually look like he was at death's door when he did so.

He shot his eyes around the room as he checked Adrian's vitals. The Komodo dragon scrambled to try to get out from behind the counter, but Twitch wouldn't let it. The shape-changing fairy was in his big pony form and stood with his hindquarters to the lizard, kicking it over and over again. It squealed and tried to get around Twitch, but there was no room and the fairy was quick as lightning, and then he kicked the lizard back into the inferno of the diner's kitchen. The lizard shrieked and disappeared.

Mike fired his M1911 and plugged a flying serpent right through the cross of its wings, breaking the beastie in half and dropping it to the floor. Next to him, Owen the accountant held another snake pinned to the table with his meaty fist. It squirmed as he sawed off its head with a steak knife. Jim smashed a snake to the wall with his tray, the last that Eddie could see, and then he threw his shoulder against the tray and squashed the reptile into paste.

Adrian had a pulse. He was breathing, too.

But his breath was ragged and shallow, his heartbeat was intermittent, and he didn't look very good.

Eddie took a deep breath and let it out. His own heart raced like a train and he felt adrenalin surge through him. He held still and tried to let himself calm down.

"That was hilarious," Twitch offered.

"Jeez," Mike said, and he laughed a shaky laugh. "You guys ever go anywhere that you don't burn to the ground?"

"What?" Owen was astonished. "You mean this kind of thing happens to you a lot?"

"It isn't on purpose," Eddie growled. He sat up, trembling. "And I wouldn't say that it happens *a lot*." Through the order window, in the burning kitchen, he saw a row of men wearing helmets, hanging from the neck by nooses and dancing in the fire. "But it has happened once or twice *lately*."

The horse disappeared and Twitch was there, head to toe in his usual spiked leathers, with his ever-present horse's tail dangling behind. "How's Adrian?" he asked.

Eddie shrugged. "I think he put himself into a coma," he said. "Anyway, you can see he looks like death warmed over, and then he cast some sort of spell and passed out."

"So, business as usual?" Mike joked.

"Maybe." Eddie shrugged again. "But he said something that might have been *Hypnos* in his incantation. Isn't that the god of sleep? I think maybe he knocked himself out before the poison could kill him."

"Spell?" Owen said. He held his big fifty caliber Desert Eagle again, carefully pointed away from everyone, like an experienced and safety-trained shooter. "Incantation? God of sleep?"

"Owen," Eddie said, feeling stiff and sore, and his scorched butt hurting him, "I just watched you saw a flying serpent in half like so much ribeye. You gonna quibble about incantations now?"

"Nope," Owen chuckled. "I guess not. But if this kind of thing happens a lot, maybe there's a market opportunity here. Have you thought about making a business out of it? I mean, monster pest removal, or something?"

"Sounds like a winner of an idea to me," Eddie agreed. "It's all yours."

"So, what?" Mike asked. "We find a cure for the poison before Adrian wakes up?"

"Or his wards of sleeping wear off. Or he just dies," Twitch agreed. "Humans are so fragile."

"Humans?" Owen asked, and then he shook his head. "Never mind."

"Adrian told me three hours," Eddie shared. "That doesn't sound like very much time to me."

"That'd just about get you to show time," the big club manager observed.

"Perfect," Eddie grunted. "Our sound really depends on those big organ chords. You got cops in this town?"

"No, but it ain't that big a county," Owen said. "Sheriff could be here sooner than you'd think."

Eddie nodded and climbed to his feet. Standing, he saw the dead trucker, and beside the trucker, the corpses of the two old ladies. They were all swollen and purple in the face. The heat scorched him, making his burned cheeks throb sympathetically, but he dragged himself around behind the counter and looked down at the corpse. At Samantha's body, he forced himself to say.

Poor girl.

At least the gnawing fangs of her unholy serpent children had hidden the mark of Eddie's bullet hole. He sighed and dug around in her pockets. Sometimes this could be the world's worst gig.

"Car keys," he announced as he found them. "Nothing else."

"We gotta get Adrian's body," Mike said, "I mean, we gotta get *Adrian* out of here."

Owen stooped to one knee and picked up the wizard in a quick, practiced fireman's carry. Eddie liked the club manager—he was a practical, can-do sort of guy. "I'll carry him across the street to the club," Owen offered. "At least until the ambulance gets here."

"No hospital is going to be able to help our organist, poor boy," Twitch observed. "Unless you mean a nunnery...? There are orders of sisters still passing down the old healing arts, though I didn't know there were any in Oklahoma."

"No, I ... what?" the accountant looked puzzled.

"Never mind," Eddie told him. "If you can take him to the club, that would be great. Don't tell anybody he's there, and don't let the EMTs get him, if you can help it. With Adrian's luck, they'd just undo his wards and kill him. We're going to have to look into this poison ourselves, and find a cure." He looked pointedly at the flames licking up along the ceiling and headed for the door.

The burly club manager pushed out the door first, not even breathing hard from his burden—Adrian was a solidly-built guy, but he was short. Mike followed, then Twitch, then Eddie, holding the car keys. Jim exited last, looking around the diner as the flames charged out of the kitchen and into the rest of the building, as if daring more snakes to show their scaly heads.

Jim was no paladin, but the guy really hated evil, and had a jones for whupping its backside whenever he could.

Speaking of backsides, Eddie's hurt. He limped into the gravel parking lot next to the diner, looking for a car in the pale afternoon sun. Pale, but really hot. Eddie would have been pathetically grateful for just two minutes of Chicago winter.

"I'll have him when you're ready," Owen grunted, and headed across the street for his club.

The town wasn't much more than a crossroads, Highway 56 and some nameless county road that cut out at right angles through the fields of dryland wheat. Everything out in this part of the world was right angles, it seemed to Eddie. Showed a lack of imagination. There wasn't a rise of land higher than six feet in sight, and the enormous watery-blue sky was broken at the margins only by about a dozen buildings. The diner was nameless, a third-rate imitation of a Denny's built entirely of plywood and now burning. Correia's across the street looked like it might once have been a barn, built of corrugated steel and windows covered in iron bars and chicken wire. The two neon signs in its windows read *BEER* and *GIRLS*. Past the bar was a combination gas station / mini-mart and then a long low building with a boardwalk and a sign that read *FEED AND SEED*. Further beyond that, past a quarter mile of weeds, Eddie saw some bulkier building, like a smallish big box store. Finally, there were other buildings scattered here and there whose uses Eddie couldn't immediately identify—houses or municipal buildings or signless businesses. They all looked like prefabricated sheds, square and ugly.

And that was the whole town.

It was easy to find Sami's vehicle. Other than the band's hammered brown Dodge van, the dusty little Camry was the only car in the parking lot.

"Start the van," Eddie told Mike. The big Mexican piled into the driver's seat and got the engine growling; Jim and Twitch followed Eddie to look at the waitress's car. "Crank the AC up as high as you can!" Eddie yelled over his shoulder as Mike ground his window open with the old-fashioned crank-style handle.

But there was nothing in the Camry. A bent pine tree freshener, a purse with a few dog-eared bucks in it, a credit card and a driver's license, and a book so creased in the spine it almost fell apart as Eddie picked it up: *Chicken Soup for the Waitress's Soul.*

"Nuts," Eddie muttered. "Check the trunk," he called to Twitch and pushed the button that opened it.

He sat in the driver's seat and leafed through the *Chicken Soup* book. It was full of stories about cute animals, and people helping each other, and good folks ground down by life who had faith and therefore things eventually went their way. Optimistic bullshit, all of it. Buy my book, because I will tell you what you want to believe, that you can change your life with the pure and holy power of your hope. Eddie snorted, but not too hard. He didn't really disdain the book, any more than he disdained its readers. He almost admired them—they were trying to put a good face on existence, trying to live happy lives.

Really, it was better that they didn't know the truth.

Eddie rummaged through the glove compartment. A compact mirror, a stub of lipstick, a ballpoint pen without a cap.

Nothing else.

"Hell." He got out of the car.

Bam, bam, bam! Mike pounded on the outside of the van's door with his fist. "Come on, man!" he shouted. "Adrian's *dying!*"

"I remember," Eddie muttered.

"Nothing in the trunk," Twitch reported. "Unless you think antifreeze will help our boy." The fairy held up a sloshing blue jug and grinned.

"Nothing in the car, either," Eddie reported. "We may be out of luck." Then he found the bookmark in the middle of *Chicken Soup*—it was a pamphlet, printed cheap on a photocopy machine on a single sheet of paper. "Hold on."

Jim loomed over him, leaning in close.

"What is it?" Mike called.

"That doesn't look Christian," Twitch observed. "Not that I'm an expert, but don't you people usually put Jesus on your pamphlets?"

Twitch was right, it didn't look Christian. *First Church of the Redeemer Nehushtan* was the title printed on the front of the pamphlet, over an image that looked like a caduceus, a snake twisted around a tall cross. Under the serpent-cross was the name *Phineas Irving, Preacher.* "Yeah," Eddie agreed. "We do."

He flipped open the pamphlet to look at the inside. There was an address and a short quotation that Eddie knew immediately: *"And these signs shall follow them that believe; In my name shall they cast out devils; they shall speak with new tongues; They shall take up serpents; and if they drink any deadly thing, it shall not hurt them: they shall lay hands on the sick, and they shall recover."*

"Mark sixteen," he said. "The pamphlet's Christian. I think."

"Bible?" Twitch asked.

"They shall take up serpents," Eddie read out loud. "They shall lay hands on the sick, and they shall recover."

"That sounds fitting," Twitch looked at the pamphlet, nodding as if he could read.

"It's Bible," Eddie said, and Jim nodded.

"It's Bible again, Mike!" Twitch called out to the band's bassist. "Wouldn't you know it?"

"Chingado," Mike grumbled. "Moses half or Jesus half?"

"Jesus half," Eddie said. "But does it matter?"

Mike shrugged. "Just saying I should have read that when I had the chance. Instead of all those comic books."

"Yeah," Eddie shot back, "you should have. But you ain't dead, so it ain't too late."

"Too late for me," Mike shook his head.

"It ain't too late," Eddie disagreed. "It ain't too late for anyone."

"Not even for the damned?" Mike asked. It wasn't an academic question, not for any of them, but Eddie let it hang. It was only mid-afternoon, and he'd already had more than enough hell and damnation to last him the day. "But what good does it do Adrian?"

Eddie noticed some scribbling at the back of the pamphlet and looked closer. *APEP*, someone had written. Next to a squiggly line. He frowned, feeling an uncomfortable nervousness at the base of his spine.

In the distance, he heard sirens. Could be the fire department, from some bigger town, or maybe the county owned fire trucks. Could be an ambulance. Could be cops. None of those would be much of a problem.

He held up the pamphlet for Jim to see. Jim shot his ice blue eyes over it quickly, and nodded.

20

"Come on," Eddie said to Twitch, and he climbed into the shotgun seat. Jim and the fairy got into the back.

Eddie set his chunky watch to a two hour, forty-five minute countdown.

"Where are we going?" Mike asked.

Eddie flipped back to the front page of the pamphlet and picked up his sawed-off shotgun. "This is your lucky day, Mike," he said. "It ain't even Sunday, and we're going to church."

CHAPTER THREE

Who's the redeemer Nehushtan?" Mike asked. The bass player was driving, but he rolled slowly through town, a little directionless, and he spared a glance for the pamphlet. "I know there's a lot of saints, but I don't think I've heard of that one. Is he one of the weird ones, like he sat on a pole for forty years or had his skin peeled off or somebody forced him to eat his own ears?"

They rolled past Correia's just as the big manager, Owen, shuffled through the bar's front door with Adrian slung across his shoulder. He winked and waved before he disappeared.

"The Nehushtan ain't a saint," Eddie said. "It's an object. Book of Numbers."

"Who knew that memorizing the Bible would be such a useful thing for the guitar player in a rock and roll band?" Twitch smirked.

"I haven't *memorized* it," Eddie grumbled. "I've just *read* it." Hadn't memorized *all* of it, anyway.

"Fine," Mike surrendered. "Next time we stay in a motel nice enough to have a Gideon in the drawer, I'll steal it. Happy?"

"Not really."

"So what is it?" Twitch asked. "Is it a snake?"

"And where are we going?" Mike asked.

The sirens and flashing lights ahead drew closer. It looked like a couple of sheriff's deputies in a pickup. "Let's ask Officer Friendly," Eddie suggested.

"Uh … what?"

Eddie leaned over from the shotgun seat, enjoying the squirt of conditioned air hitting his face from the slits in the dashboard, weak as it was, and jammed his hand on the horn. Mike braked, the van shuddering to a halt, and the truck slowed to meet them.

"Twitch," Eddie warned the fairy he was at bat.

"Got it," Twitch said.

Mike and the driver of the sheriff's truck both rolled their windows down. The deputy was a sour-faced man with thick eyebrows.

"You got something to tell us about the fire, son," he said gruffly to Mike, "you'd better not leave the scene." The truck was in neutral but he revved the engine, making the point that he was on official business and in a hurry.

Twitch leaned over Mike's shoulder, taking on a more feminine look. It had taken Eddie a good long while to get used to the way the fairy shifted back and forth between male and female, and then was sometimes an animal, but he thought nothing of it anymore.

"We're not going anywhere, deputy," Twitch said. "We're parked right here, waiting for you." He winked.

"Right," the deputy grunted, pleased. He pulled up the truck's handbrake. "And what do you know about the fire?" He seemed to have completely forgotten that there actually was a fire, even as he was discussing it. Whatever training should have sent him to the conflagration to rescue people in peril, direct traffic, or whatever, evaporated under the direct assault of Twitch's Glamour.

"The snake did it," Twitch smiled. "A snake in the kitchen."

"Did you manage to get your hands on the snake?" the second deputy leered. He was heavier, and wore a cowboy hat and a mustache.

"Easy," Eyebrows objected. "She's a lady." Eddie almost laughed out loud at that one. Whatever the deputy was seeing, it wasn't the silver-haired drummer in black leather and spikes. And he definitely wasn't seeing the horse's tail.

Jim shifted impatiently.

"Address, Twitch," Eddie muttered from the shotgun seat. "Adrian's dying, remember."

"I'm new to town, gentlemen," Twitch said to the two lawmen, "and I'm looking for someone. His name is—" he took the pamphlet from Eddie, "Phineas Irving, and his address—"

"Crazy son of a bitch," said Mustache.

"You one of his weirdos, then?" asked Eyebrows. "I mean, parishioners?"

"We get complaints," Mustache said darkly. "Snake worshippers, or some crazy nonsense like that, and laying on of hands," he practically slobbered at the words, "I think we all know what *that* means."

"He's my cousin," Twitch lied smoothly. "I'm just visiting."

Eyebrows jerked a thumb over his own shoulder in the direction of the big box store. "Turn right at the Sears," he said. "Nothing else out there but your cousin and the rattlesnakes."

"You've been very helpful," Twitch batted his eyes at the deputies. "I'm sorry you won't remember anything about me."

"Me, too," Mustache grinned, thinking he was still flirting.

Eddie tapped Mike's shoulder. "That's your cue," he whispered, and Mike put the van into gear. The deputies waved like excited little kids as the Dodge rolled forward and they disappeared from view.

"Ugh," Twitch flopped back onto his seat. "Two men at the same time is so exhausting."

Mike gulped and kept his eyes on the road.

"Only two?" Eddie chuckled. "It looked to me like you had Mike here going, too."

Twitch yawned and stretched himself. "That's our Mikey," he said. "Excitable boy."

"Mike," the bass player muttered. "Call me Mike." He looked a little grumpy, and Jim slapped him on the shoulder to cheer him up.

Eddie turned from his band mates, saw the Sears—
and was stunned.

Ice swept the ground around the blocky retailer, thick and bleak as a Minnesota lake in winter, with bodies stuck in it. Faces emerged from the ice, hundreds of them dotting the frozen plain like geese on a pond. Blue lips moaned soundlessly, and a bitter wind ripped through and around the heads, whipping up crystal flurries of snow and ice, tearing at their ears and noses and ripping away bits of flesh.

Eddie was grateful for the burns on his bum. Their grinding pain reminded him that the vision was just a vision.

"Damn," he shuddered and looked away, rubbing his eyes.

"Where do I turn?" Mike asked, and Eddie had to look back. "There's only a parking lot."

He still saw the sheet of ice and the tortured heads. The sight of it hurt Eddie, and it frightened him. His glimpses of Hell were constant, but they were rarely sustained. He saw a person or a small knot of people being tortured by Azazel's minions and then his vision passed on. He never saw this many, and he never held a vision this long.

"Am I the only one seeing this?" he asked.

Mike shrugged. "What, the crappy run down Sears with the dirt parking lot and no right turn?" he asked, and then he understood. "Oh."

"I'm the only one," Eddie said.

"*Carajo,*" Mike said by way of expressing sympathy.

Eddie couldn't look, and he couldn't really keep from looking. He would have sworn the heads were looking back at him, and he felt naked and guilty. He saw the damned all the time, but the damned never saw him. What was this vision? What was this place? He shrank within himself, and then he realized something was tapping on his shoulder.

It was Jim. The singer reached past Eddie now and pointed. Out his Infernal Eye, Eddie saw only the glacier of the damned and the wind that gnawed at their heads, but if he concentrated on the other eye, he thought he saw a dirt road exiting the parking lot at its far end. He pointed too, hesitant and uncertain.

"I see it," Mike said, and turned the van into the lot.

The heads stared at Eddie as he drove through. His vision was silent, but the frost-furred lips and bluing flesh were so vivid, he imagined he could hear the crumbling, terrified moans of the damned souls. Eyes sunk deep into black pits, their lashes ripped away by the frozen wind, rolled in their sockets to stare at him as the Dodge trundled across the parking lot. They were so close, and so many, and had been there so long, that Eddie began to feel *cold*.

And then they were gone, and the van was back in the griddle-hot and griddle-flat desert of the Oklahoma panhandle, rattling along a dirt road between two fields of burnt-brown wheat stalks.

Eddie sucked in a deep breath and let it out slowly.

"What the hell is wrong with that Sears?" he asked.

"I dunno," Mike shrugged. "Jeez, you tell me."

"I ... I ..." Eddie groped blindly. "I don't know. There was something really bad there." He kneed open the glove compartment, took out a box of bullets and started reloading the Glock's emptied clips. The ammunition ritual gave him a little tactile comfort, but no distraction. He wished he had a cup of hot coffee to sip.

"Is it following us?" Twitch asked.

Eddie looked back over his shoulder, past gig bags, amps and stacks of Adrian's electronic gizmos and through the rear windows. He saw only desert.

"No," he dropped himself into his seat and sighed. "Forget it."

"Yeah," Mike agreed, "forget it. Tell me about the Nehushtan."

"It was a snake," Eddie spat out, trying to block the images of the frozen damned from his mind's eye.

"Following us?" Twitch asked. "A snake at the Sears?"

"No," Eddie said. "I mean the Nehushtan. You're right, Twitch, it was a snake. A snake on a stick. The Israelites in the desert, they were bitten, the Bible says, by a bunch of fiery serpents."

"Moses half," Mike said, like it was an important insight.

"Moses half, the Israelites after they left Egypt. Like with Charlton Heston. And Moses put a snake on a stick and raised it up, and when the Israelites looked at it they were healed. That snake was the Nehushtan."

"They were healed of their snake bites," Mike concluded. "Adrian was bitten by a snake."

"And this guy's church says it's the church of the Redeemer Nehushtan," Eddie said. "It can't be a coincidence that it's here. It can't be a coincidence that the waitress ... Sami, it can't be a coincidence that she had this pamphlet in her car."

"Could be he's the one who knocked her up," Twitch suggested cheerfully.

"Could be she was going to him for help," Mike had a different take. "What was that Bible bit you read on it? People holding snakes and not getting bitten, or something? Lay on hands and heal people?"

"Either way," Eddie growled, "it's the right place to start looking for a cure. Or maybe it's the right place to start looking for the problem, which is sometimes the same thing. Only I don't know what this other thing is." He turned the pamphlet over and read the end of it again. "Apep."

"Oh, that's easy," said Twitch. "That's not from the Bible."

"I know that," Eddie rumbled. "So what is it?" He saw a row of naked men, pinned to the road in front of the Dodge with long jagged wooden spikes like thorns through their bellies. The van rolled over them with the same bumping it made on the dirt road, and Eddie was glad for the new vision of torment—it was brief, and it almost helped him forget the frozen Hell-Sears.

Almost.

"Apep is one of the Egyptians," Twitch said lightly. "He's a snake, as it happens."

"Or maybe not just *as it happens*," Eddie countered. "*Snakes* seem to be the order of the day."

"*Mierda.*"

"Right." Twitch considered. "Well, that's not good. He's not thought of as one of the good ones, not even by the Egyptians, and you know how crazy they can be. Bird-headed men and dogs with aardvark snouts and all that crazy mixing up of forms." He grinned mischievously. "Hilarious."

"What does he do?" Eddie asked.

"Ah ..." Twitch thought. "I don't know. Eats people. He's a giant snake, what do giant snakes do? Shed giant skin? Dance for giant flute players? Live under giant sheds?"

"So we got an Egyptian snake god on a pamphlet printed by a guy who preaches under the sign of the snake, which we found in the car of a woman who gave birth to a bunch of snakes that ate her alive." Eddie grabbed the Remington 870, checked its magazine and shoved a handful of shells into his pocket. "That about sum it up?"

"And Adrian was bitten by a snake," Twitch reminded him.

Jim pointed again. At the top of a very slight rise sagged a dilapidated yellow and blue double-wide trailer. Above it, a tilted rusty weathervane rooster dawdled lazily back and forth, and to one side, half-collapsed and leaning right up against the wall of the trailer, slouched a big dirty canvas tent. At the start of the dirt track that turned off and led to the trailer, a sheet of plywood hung nailed to a lashed tripod of two-by-fours. On the plywood was painted a ragged cross, and a long snake coiled around it, meeting the viewer's gaze with beady eyes and flickering tongue.

"Friendly," Mike joked.

"Cheerful!" Twitch added.

"Better than Sears," Eddie shot back. "Best park the van here. We don't want to go in guns blazing, in case we need this guy's help."

Mike stopped the van and they piled out. Jim took his sword this time, buckling its belt around his waist right over his jeans. Twitch looked unarmed, but he was always able to produce those wooden batons he used both to play the drums and to pound the minions of Hell over the head. Mike had the .45 semi-auto he'd picked up in New Mexico tucked into his belt; as an afterthought, he grabbed a knife out of the driver's side door pocket and stuck it in his pants.

It was Eddie's van, more or less, and he tried to keep it full of weapons. It was easy enough, when you didn't really have to worry about questions from the cops.

Eddie carried the Glock in its shoulder holster and the Remington hanging off a sling. His old green jacket's pockets were stuffed full of things that could be useful, too, though most of them weren't weapons per se—pocket knives, a compass, string, a deck of playing cards, matches, duct tape, that sort of thing. The duct tape especially came in handy when you played in the kind of band where your gear was always falling apart. He had a couple of odd knick-knacks that really just had emotional value, too, he could admit to himself, like a plastic cup full of jacks and a red bouncing ball. In a pinch, he could kill a person with any one of those things, if nothing else, by stuffing them down the poor bastard's throat.

Even the jacks.

Giant snake gods, he was less sure about.

The afternoon sun hammered down hot, despite a stiff desert breeze that came and went, thick with the scent of sagebrush. "I got point," he told the others, "and Mike's got the rear. Keep an eye on the van. Twitch, get overhead and give it a look." He turned and headed out.

He heard Twitch's sharp cry as the fairy sprang into the air, and the silver falcon's horse's tail brushed Eddie's head as he took flight, racing up the gentle slope and towards the trailer. Twitch was pretty—though kind of weird—as a bird, but Eddie had seen it before, and kept his attention focused. For all that he didn't want to kick in the door, he didn't want to get caught with his pants around his ankles either, so he walked with the Remington in his hand, pointed down at the ground but ready to pull up and shoot if he needed it.

Eddie was calm, and normally he trusted his own judgment and coolness. He still felt a bit shaken by his vision of the backcountry Sears, though. He worried he might see frozen heads sticking out the ground and feel like he had to shoot them.

Instead, he heard a hiss and a rattle off to his right. He turned, brought up the stubby nose of the shotgun and almost fired, anyway.

But Jim got there first. With a loud *snick!* his sword jumped from its scabbard and the head of the rattlesnake snapped off and went flying into the brush. The snake's body, scaly yellow-brown and surprisingly long, danced spastically before collapsing into the dust.

And then suddenly there were two more snakes lifting their heads from the dust to threaten Jim. The big singer kicked one incoming with his boot, sending it sailing into the back of the church's plywood sign with a loud, meaty *thud*. The second lost its head like its companion.

"*Huevos!*"

And then there were a dozen.

"Twitch!" Eddie yelled.

So much for the quiet approach. Eddie pumped the shotgun and waded into the hissing curtain of rattlesnakes.

Boom! went Eddie's shotgun. *Snick!* followed Jim's sword. And then Mike finally got his gun out of his pants and joined in, *bang! bang! bang!*

"I don't like this!" Eddie shouted, stepping over spattered snake meat to take aim at another serpent, blasting it to oblivion.

Jim nodded and pointed up at the trailer by way of answer. He skewered two rattlesnakes with a single deft stab of his blade and then scraped them off with the instep of his heavy boot.

Mike saw Jim's gesture and led the way, jogging up the track towards the trailer. He got ahead of Eddie, who took a couple of seconds to turn around and follow, but Eddie could tell by Mike's continued shots, and the plumes of dirt that exploded into the air around the bass player, that he was still threatened by attacking snakes.

Jim brought up the rear. Eddie didn't worry much about him, and worried even less when Twitch swooped down suddenly from the blue sky to snatch up a pair of snakes, one in each claw.

Mike, though, looked like he was in trouble. Snakes closed in on him from behind, and on both right and left, as he staggered over a cattle guard and between two driftwood fence posts. He fired again and then dug into his pocket for his second clip.

The big guy stumbled—

Eddie whipped up his shotgun and broke into a run as snakes swarmed out of the tall dry grass and sage, slithering towards the bass player on the ground—

and then a wave of gray-brown fur washed over Mike. Something like a dog—several things that looked like dogs, or maybe foxes, it was hard to tell at this distance—scurried over Mike's back and legs and threw themselves at the snakes.

Something was helping Mike. That gave Eddie the breathing room he needed to blast a couple of rattlers out of his own way, and then he was on top of the bass player, grabbing Mike by his elbow and dragging him to his feet.

"*Cojón!*" Mike shouted. Jim caught up with them and they raced for the double-wide. Bouncing blue and yellow in his jogging vision, the little building didn't look cheerful at all—it looked ominous and false, like a clown's greasepaint smile. The trailer sat on blocks, Eddie saw, and was hugged by a rough wraparound plank porch. Under the trailer was darkness, and he wondered if there were more snakes lurking. And if there weren't, what was lurking inside? Was Phineas Irving, preacher, some kind of snake-summoning warlock, sending his minions at them by mind control?

But zigzagging lines were chopped into the planks of the porch, and though Eddie saw snakes coiling and sliding on the ground right up to the edge of the wood, he noticed that none of them actually so much as touched the planks.

"What are those things, badgers?" Mike shot at another snake. "Ferrets?"

"You'd have been a great farmer, Mike," Eddie laughed. Jim swiped with his sword and swept three snakes out of the way, clearing a path to the porch. Eddie and Mike charged through, with the singer on their heels, and then they spun to look at the field of snakes behind them.

Twitch the falcon snatched another snake from the ground, tearing it in half with his talons and shattering its skull with his beak. The gray-brown things, whatever they were, played havoc with the snakes. They had long faces and bodies and tails but stubby little ears, and they were quick as bullets, slipping out under every rattler's strike and then biting snakes through their windpipes, killing them instantly.

"Weasels?" Eddie guessed. It had been a long time since he'd earned his Mammals merit badge. Whatever these things were, he hadn't seen any in Chicago. Or Iraq. He kept the Remington trained on the snakes nearest him—just because they hadn't come on the porch yet didn't mean they couldn't or wouldn't do so now. But the rattlers hissed, shook their tails at him, showed him their long, curving fangs, and stayed back.

Twitch alighted beside the three of them, melting into his human form. He chose his female shape, which Eddie assumed was for Mike's benefit and the amusement it gave the fairy, because Mike saw Twitch and did a double-take. "Whatever it is," Twitch hazarded, "it isn't cats."

"Cats?" Mike asked.

"Mongoose," said a voice Eddie didn't know, and he realized the colossal screw-up he'd just committed. "Hands up."

Eddie relaxed his grip on the shotgun, letting it dangle by its strap from his right shoulder. He raised his hands over his head, his companions doing the same, and they turned to look at the source of the voice.

The man was tall and wiry, the kind of wiriness you got by living in the desert and not taking in enough water or calories. The skin of his face and his big knuckles was sunburned and rubbed raw by the wind, and a shock of bristly yellow hair made his head look like a scrub brush. A once-nice gray wool suit jacket hung off him like a trench coat off a scarecrow. He squinted down the barrel of an M1917 Enfield into Eddie's chest. That would be a .30-06 cartridge, Eddie knew, and it would blow a hole in him the size of a pineapple.

"You Phineas Irving, by any chance?" Eddie asked.

CHAPTER FOUR

I 'm the owner of this land," the scarecrow spat out. "And you're trespassers." His elbow was a little jittery, but his aim didn't waver.

"Mierda."

"Easy," Eddie said. "We didn't come looking for a fight." Jim looked poised to stab the guy; that he hadn't done it yet probably meant he took seriously the threat that the homeowner would kill Eddie.

"You have guns out," the blond man pointed out. "You're shooting."

"At snakes!" Eddie snapped, exasperated. "Didn't you notice you're surrounded?"

The gunman dropped his elbows to his sides and seemed to relax, just a little. The gray-brown animals bounded up onto the porch and cuddled around his ankles. "Yeah," he said, "but the fact that you're carrying them at all makes me nervous. And your friend has a sword."

Jim's nostrils flared menacingly.

"He's old-fashioned," Eddie said. "And this is Oklahoma. Aren't we required by law to carry guns?"

The man grunted and considered. "I'm Irving," he admitted. "What do you want?"

"Can we talk?" Eddie suggested. Irving hadn't shot him when he had the chance, which made him think the preacher might not be a bad guy. "We're just looking for a little information."

"Put down the guns," Irving countered. "And the sword. And if the fairy talks, I start shooting."

Eddie was a little unsettled that Phineas Irving had spotted Twitch for a fairy. It probably meant that he had seen Twitch transform himself from falcon form. And it definitely meant that he knew enough about the real nature of the world not to be freaked out at the thought of fairies. And he knew that if Twitch talked, he might pull out the Glamour.

But he unslung the shotgun and laid it on the planks, and Mike and Jim followed his lead.

Eddie didn't mention the Glock.

"You preach under the sign of the serpent," Eddie observed. "But it's the raised serpent, the one that heals snakebite."

"Oh?"

"The Nehushtan."

"You know your Old Testament," Irving conceded. He kept the rifle pointed at Eddie's chest. "Or you read the signboard. Good for you. How did you find me and what's the information you want?"

"If I could just reach into my pocket?" Eddie waited for the preacher's slight nod, and he pulled out the church brochure. He unfolded it and showed it to Irving.

"You friends of Sami's?" There was a note of concern in the man's voice. "How is she?"

"How did you know that was Sami's?" Mike sounded impressed. "What, did you only print one of them?"

"I only *wrote on* one of them." Irving nodded at the squiggle and the name *APEP*.

"You got the drop on us," Eddie noted calmly, "and either way we need your help. Maybe you'd better tell us whose side you're on."

Phineas Irving chuckled bitterly. "Choose you this day," he quoted.

"Joshua," Eddie said. "Moses half," he added, for Mike's benefit.

"As for me and my house," Irving nodded at the plywood sign of the Nehushtan, "we will serve the Lord."

"And Apep?" Eddie asked.

"Sami had a … a problem," Irving said. "She came to me, and I tried to help her."

"I think she gave birth to her problem," Mike grunted. "And it ate her. Not to mention a lot of other people, almost including us."

"Dammit."

"Yeah," Eddie agreed. "Flying poisonous snakes. *Dammit* is right."

"And you?" Irving asked. "The snakes wanted to bite you, so you're not one of theirs. Whose side are *you* on?"

"Mostly," Eddie told him, "we're on our own side. But we have a problem, and I think we need your help."

Irving looked at the four of them, his inspection lingering on Twitch. "Are you telling me the fairy's pregnant?" he asked.

"Ew!" Twitch snorted.

Irving failed to make good his threat, and shot no one. Eddie noticed the omission, and relaxed a few degrees.

"I'm telling you that our buddy … our organ player, actually, got bitten by one of … one of Sami's problems."

"When?"

Eddie checked his watch. "About half an hour ago."

"Then your friend is dead."

"He might be," Eddie agreed, "but he might not. He's a wizard, and he put himself into some kind of magical coma right after he was bitten. I think he meant to slow down the poison, and I'm hoping it worked. But it won't mean anything if we don't find a cure."

"You're hoping that because I have the Nehushtan raised over my church that I can cure your friend," Irving finished the thought. He didn't bat an eye at the word *wizard*.

"Yeah," Mike said.

"Pick up your weapons," Phineas Irving said, "and come inside."

"Can I talk now?" Twitch asked impishly.

"Depends on what you say," Irving answered. He patted the stock of his rifle affectionately, like he was patting a baby's bum. "I'm still armed."

The inside of the trailer was an unholy mess, but not the kind of mess Eddie expected. There was no sign of drugs or booze or personal filth, and it smelled okay, but the trailer was full of books and papers in total disarray. It was like a library-meteorite had hit inside and exploded, scattering handwritten notes and diagrams all over the place. The linoleum countertop and the plastic coffee table and the sunken-centered couches fraying at the shoulders were all barely visible under snowdrifts of paper.

"Read much?" Mike asked.

"Not enough," Irving said grimly. He gestured at the couches. "Shove that stuff onto the table. Coffee?"

"Please." Eddie meant it. He and Jim shoveled papers aside so the band could sit down. He sat on the nearest couch and sank deeply into it—the couch was ugly, but worn to the perfect point of comfort. But for the scorched skin of his backside, the couch might have put him to sleep.

"I'll put on a fresh pot."

"Screw that," Eddie said. "Gimme the coffee. Black."

"I'll take sugar, cream, whatever you got," Mike added.

"When my brother and I fell out," the preacher recounted, pouring coffee into chipped mugs, "it was over a woman."

"Isn't it always?" Mike grunted.

"I totally wanna hear your life story," Eddie said. "It sounds like country music, and I am definitely a fan of Nashville. First, can you tell me how to help my friend?"

"I'm telling you now," Irving said, shuffling slowly across the scabby shag floor with mugs in his fists. He was a little shaky, but he managed not to spill. It didn't escape Eddie's notice that he'd left the rifle in the kitchenette. "It's the woman. And *fell out* is something of an understatement."

Eddie took the coffee. It smelled bitter and the warm mug stung his burned hands at the touch. He took a sip and felt strengthened. "Ah," he sighed, "acid for the battery. Go on."

"Her name was Miriam," the preacher said. He drew up a three-legged stool and settled his lanky frame onto it. His pets flopped down on the floor next to him and wrestled each other. "Maybe it still is. I loved her very much."

Jim snorted. It was a cynical sound.

"Don't talk much, do you?" Irving asked the singer.

"He's cursed," Eddie said. It was sort of a lie, but it was much simpler than trying to explain the whole story. "So this woman of yours, Miriam, she can heal snakebite?"

"Jeez," Mike muttered, "you don't know how to tell a story. Get to the part where something happens already."

Irving ignored both of them. "I was an Egyptologist," he said, and then he chuckled wryly. "Who am I kidding? I was a grad student at Penn, studying to be an Egyptologist. I was going to be to the next Flinders Petrie. I was doing physical archaeology, potsherds and garbage heaps. Miriam was in my program. She was doing the sexier stuff, the Coffin Texts and Old Kingdom demonology. She was young and beautiful and I fell in love. I thought we both did. We got engaged."

Eddie saw a man and a woman, naked, standing behind the preacher. They were emaciated, their hair falling out. Each held a jagged saw to the other's abdomen and yanked back and forth on the handle. Blood gushed down, drenching their legs. He resisted the urge to make fun of the man for the romance in his story. "Go on."

"My brother Aaron was studying theology," Irving continued. "He became obsessed with old gnostic documents about apotheosis, the divinization of man. Crazy stuff, all about men becoming like the gods, or becoming angels."

"Yeah, crazy," Mike muttered.

"And it was all in Coptic, so he and Miriam spent a lot of time together."

"But in these gnostic books," Eddie probed, "in the Coffin Texts or whatever, Miriam learned how to deal with these flying snakes? Where is she? Is she in town here?"

"She's close," Irving said dryly. "While we were engaged, she and Aaron became lovers. When I ... found out about it, when she told me about it, you know, she said it had nothing to do with love, and nothing to do with me, it had to do with the ritual."

"So you called it off," Mike concluded. "Sent the skank packing."

"What ritual?" Eddie asked.

"They wanted to summon Apep, but there were steps they had to take before that, to become his true worshippers. To get his gifts.

Apep's a snake god—well, a snake *devil*, really—and his worship is orgiastic, so they … they became involved."

"Isn't that your family, Jim?" Twitch asked. "I mean, aren't you all cousins or something, according to Eddie? Family reunions must be so entertaining."

Jim glowered at the drummer and drew his sword partly out of the sheath, exposing six inches of sharp blade.

"But why on earth would they want to summon the big snake?" Twitch asked, ignoring the bared weapon. The fairy looked more curious than shocked. "There are easier ways to commit suicide."

"Power, I think," Irving said wearily. "And immortality."

"The snake sheds its skin, born anew each time," Eddie whispered to himself. "Are they crazy? Can they possibly be right?"

"I think both," Phineas Irving said. "I found out on our honeymoon. I woke up in the middle of the night in the hotel and she was gone, so I rang her cell phone. When I heard it in the room next door, I broke in and found them." He stopped talking and his eyes glazed over. His face was drawn and pale.

"Orgiastic, you said." Mike fidgeted. He stared at the mongooses, tussling and tossing each other about on the trailer's shag carpet. "Does that mean what it sounds like?"

"What does it sound like?" Twitch winked.

Mike hesitated. "Like *orgy* plus *fantastic*."

"You mean like *ginormous*," Eddie snorted. "*Giant* plus *enormous*."

"Yes," Irving whispered, and looked down at the floor. "That's about what it means."

Eddie respected the other man's pain and waited.

"There were snakes everywhere," the Egyptologist said slowly. "And incense, a cloud of it so thick I couldn't see or breathe. And then I saw a light … like a gap in the air, and on the other side of it was lightning. And when the hole was gone, there was a crowd of people chanting and shaking rattles. And in the middle, there they were. Only … only …" He couldn't seem to get it out, whatever it was.

"Only they were snakes," Twitch guessed. "Snakes and humans at the same time, all mixed up, like the Egyptians like to do."

Eddie felt sick. "Monsters."

Irving nodded miserably. "Aaron's arms were gone, and instead he had snakes growing out of his shoulders. Once the incense cleared and the light was gone, I could see it clearly, because he was naked. And Miriam ..."

"Miriam got what she wanted," Twitch said. The fairy's voice was gentle. Eddie thought that was pretty generous of him, since only a few minutes earlier Phineas Irving had threatened to shoot Twitch if he opened his mouth.

"Miriam is a lamia," Irving told them. He couldn't meet their eyes, and just sat staring a hole into the carpet.

Mike looked baffled.

"Lower half of a snake," Eddie said. "Upper half of a woman. Ugh. Sorry, man. I didn't know you could *become* one."

"Jeez, I really gotta read the Bible one of these days." Mike shook his head in amazement.

"Snakes for hair, too," the preacher said. "Aaron and their ... cultists ... wanted to kill me, but Miriam stopped them. She told me what she'd been doing, and let me go."

"And *then* you divorced the bitch," Mike said. "'Cause a snake ... Jeez ..."

Phineas Irving shook his head. "She spared me. Besides, I was in love with her. I'm still in love with her now." He dug into the pocket of his jacket and pulled out a creased and folded letter envelope. He shook out its contents, and a single gold ring, heavy and dull, fell into his palm.

"Did they summon Apep, then?" Twitch asked.

"They're still trying," Irving said. He clenched his fists together in a big ball of knuckles around the wedding ring. "And I followed them here to try to stop them."

"That's why you're penned in by snakes?" Mike asked. "They know you're here?"

"They know I'm here," Irving agreed. "I keep the snakes at bay with my mongooses and my jerry-rigged charms. I preach against them, but the county thinks I'm crazy, so they send deputies and social workers to harass me. Almost no one listens, anyway. I try to help people I can—people like Sami, who get involved with the cult and then want to leave—and I try to figure out how to stop the summoning. They don't care. They sit just down the road and laugh at me."

"Down the road?" Mike asked.

Jim sat up, suddenly alert and looking curiously at Eddie. Even the mongooses stopped wrestling, and their stubby round ears perked up.

The hair on the back of Eddie's neck prickled. "Sears," he said. "Tell me they're not in that old shitbucket Sears we passed."

Irving just nodded.

Eddie felt a thick lump at the back of his throat. "I was hoping you'd say that you can raise up the Nehushtan on a pole and Adrian would look at it and be cured," he said. "Like in the Bible. Now you're telling me that your ... wife ... is a lamia, and she knows the cure."

Irving shook his head. "She doesn't *know* the cure."

Eddie scratched his head. "Then my memory's shorting out on me, or I just don't get it. You said *it's the woman.*"

"She doesn't *know* the cure. She *is* the cure."

"There's no Nehushtan?" Eddie pressed. "You just put up a signboard to announce that you're a snake hater?"

"There's a Nehushtan," Phineas said, and he jerked his head at the back door of the double-wide. "It's in the tent, and it might even be *the* Nehushtan. But I've never cured anybody with it. I've got enough juice to keep snakes out of the tent, and that's about it."

"Juice?" Twitch asked.

"The Nehushtan is powered by faith," Irving said. "Faith's not my strong suit." He put the ring back into the envelope and jammed it into his pocket again. "Snakes do stay out of the tent when I'm preaching, though, so that's good."

"Huevos."

"So what's the cure?" Eddie asked, slightly puzzled. "Is this some kind of voodoo thing, like the snakes are her offspring and so you can cure the children's bites with some of the mother's blood? Hair of the dog?"

"They're not her children," Irving grouched. "They're Aaron's."

Eddie felt sick. "You mean it's still an orgiastic cult," he said. "And girls like Sami ..."

Irving nodded. "Young girls, girls alone who need jobs and help," he finished. "They get taken in and ... they get taken. Boys, too. By Aaron, or by someone else in the cult. They're all monsters, or they want to become monsters. And some of the kids escape, I try to help if I can. But if they don't, then their bodies are consumed by their children. And by the other worshippers of the snake."

Mike looked shaken.

"What do you mean, you try to help?" Eddie demanded. "How did you *help* that poor girl? She was still stuck in this town, right next to the temple of the snake. Why didn't you get her out?"

Irving buried his face in his hands. "She was going to leave tomorrow," he muttered, and ran his fingers through his bristly hair. "Collect her last paycheck and leave. And I thought I had hexed her womb, killed the snakes inside. I thought she'd get to her aunt's house in Dallas and be in for a terrible shock when she delivered dead snakes ... she'd make the *National Enquirer*, but she'd be alive."

"She didn't know," Eddie realized. He remembered how delighted Sami had seemed when she thought her baby was kicking. "She thought her baby was just a normal human kid. She wanted a boy."

"Should I have told her?" Irving had despair in his face. "Would you want your daughter to know that she had snakes in her womb? I did what I could, and I thought I had done enough. I thought the danger was controlled."

"Your hex failed," Twitch said sharply. It was an awfully direct statement from the fairy, Eddie thought, and unusually judgmental.

The mongooses hissed. They chased their own tails and looked skittishly into the corners of the room.

"Jeez, are there any wizards who actually know what they're doing?" Mike asked.

"Not me," Irving said. "I'm no wizard, I'm just an Egyptologist. Not even that, I'm ABD, never got my degree. Whatever I know, I learned by reading the old monuments, execration texts, second millennium B.C. medical treatises. Or from folklore. Some of it works. I think the hex I put on this house works—anyway, the snakes don't come in."

"Anyway, it ain't a house," Mike grumbled. "It's an advertisement for meth lab tenants."

"And the Nehushtan?" Eddie asked. "You get the instructions for that out of a book?"

"I stole it. The University had it in its museum collection, and I had access because of the work I was doing on the Wadi Hammamat grave finds. I took it with me when I left. I don't know if it's authentic or not—neither did they, it was a recent acquisition and they were still examining it. But it works. At least, sort of."

"You and Adrian have a lot in common, really," Mike mused. "You a napper?"

"What?"

"What are you doing to stop the summoning?" Eddie asked. He knew this was a distraction, and that he should be focused on his real challenge—Adrian, the ticking clock, and getting the wizard cured—but the thought that some sort of snake-worshipping sex cult was trying to *summon* its demon-deity caught his attention. "Was that the idea behind stealing the Nehushtan?"

"Yeah," Irving looked depressed. "But I can barely get it to flicker. It's the real deal, all right—but I'm not. Funny thing is, if our positions were switched, Aaron could probably use it like a flamethrower. He was always a believer."

"Still is," Eddie pointed out. "Just in the wrong stuff."

Irving nodded. "And the spells. The summoning—I *think*—is a sort of group performance and incantation. I only saw it the one time, of course … on my honeymoon … but some of the kids I've known have told me that the same kind of thing is what they experienced. I think I have some ideas about how to throw a monkey wrench into it, but I'd need to have access to their props and scripts beforehand. Well," he chuckled uneasily, "or else I'd need to be present at the ritual."

"Would that be another orgy?" Mike asked.

"Boobs," Twitch said cheerfully. Mike turned his palms up in an innocent shrug and Jim shook his head in mock frustration. "We all know what you like, is all I'm saying," the drummer added.

"Yes," Irving answered. "And at the end of the orgy, Apep is supposed to appear. Surviving worshippers will be touched by him—like Aaron and Miriam were touched."

"You mean they'll turn into freaky snake-mutants," Mike interpreted. "Dare to dream."

"Surviving?" Eddie asked.

"Most of the worshippers will be eaten."

"And what do you get out of all this?" Eddie asked. "Don't go quoting the Book of Joshua and telling me you're on the Lord's side. What is it you want here? You think this gets you to Heaven?"

Irving shrugged and looked down at his feet. "Maybe," he admitted. "If there is a Heaven. Or maybe I get my revenge. Or maybe I get my wife back."

Mike whistled. "Really? Don't you just hate her too much now?"

Eddie shook his head; he understood Phineas Irving all too well. "Says the man who ain't never been married. Love and hate ain't opposites," he told the bass player. "They're pretty near the same thing. The opposite of *both* of them is just not giving a crap."

"I give a crap," Irving agreed, but he couldn't look up.

The mongooses darted across the room and through a doggie flap in the trailer door. Jim stood and stared at the animals, his hand on his sword, but the preacher waved him down.

"They're going after snakes," Phineas Irving said. "There are always snakes."

"I'm glad you care," Eddie said, and he meant it. He hoped Irving succeeded, but he was concentrating again on his own immediate problem. He wanted to get Adrian back on his feet, play the evening's gig, and get clean out of Oklahoma. "But I'm on a clock and you still haven't answered the question I care about. How does the lamia ... Mrs. Irving ... cure snakebite?"

"Milk," Irving said. "Lamia's milk is a sovereign remedy against the bite of any snake."

Twitch laughed. "Boobs," he said again.

CRACK!

The trailer shook.

CHAPTER FIVE

Eddie spilled his coffee on his lap.

"Dammit!" he yelled, and jumped to his feet. Now he was burned front and back.

Jim was already standing, and the big man whipped out his sword and raced for the door. Twitch would have been on his heels, but the drummer got tangled up in Mike, whose knees knocked the fairy down and slowed them both. The snake preacher fell off his stool with the shuddering of the trailer, and then turned and scrambled for the kitchenette, going for his Enfield rifle.

Eddie grabbed the Remington and pumped it.

The trailer shook again.

Jim opened the door and jumped back—

a snake head jammed itself at the singer, a snake head the size of a whole ham, with a tongue as long as a human arm.

Eddie saw his shot and took it. *Boom!* The Remington's slug bit into the hinge of the serpent's jaw with a small splash of blood, and the snake pulled back.

"Is that Apep?" Mike yelled. The bass player pushed the sofa over onto its back and crouched behind it, drawing his pistol and covering the windows. From the yard, Eddie heard a surprisingly loud hissing sound.

Twitch flashed into a silver avian blur and swooped out the open door. Jim fended off a second lunge of the enormous snake's head by sliding his backside up onto the kitchenette counter, kicking with the heels of both boots. Eddie scooted to the front window of the trailer, trying to get a better look outside.

The preacher came over by the kitchenette sink with the .30-06 and looked through greasy Venetian blinds at the yard. "No," he said. "Apep should be much, much bigger. Also, I think Apep should be a straightforward serpent."

Eddie brushed aside dingy cotton flaps that served as curtains with the nose of his shotgun and threw a glance into the yard. "Hell," he said.

A shambling crew of monsters rammed themselves against the porch. The mongooses stood on hind legs and hissed a protest, but the furry little snake-eaters were out of their depth here, because their foes weren't simple snakes. They were *snake-men*. The big head that shoved at the trailer door trying to get in sprouted from the shoulders of heavy-bellied human body in denim overalls. A second monster looked like a mass of snakes, an entire hedge of them, sprouting out of a brown gabardine skirt and a pair of shapely legs. A third beast was a snake the size of a Christmas tree, with three sets of muscular human arms sprouting out of its scaly flanks and a human head. There were more, but Eddie stopped cataloguing and started shooting.

Boom! Boom!

He shattered the window and put as many slugs as he could into Overalls the snake-headed man. In the yard, Twitch harassed the other serpent-thugs, but he wasn't very effective in falcon form against creatures so large. He did manage to pluck several heads off Lady Legs the bush of serpents, but either Lady Legs grew them back immediately, or she had so many to start with that the loss of a few made no difference.

Mike crawled over to join Eddie, while Phineas Irving smashed out the window over the kitchenette sink and poked the muzzle of the Enfield out through the hole. Jim slashed and stabbed at the creatures, making Overalls bleed from several chest wounds and reducing Many Arms to One Arm Less, but the monsters didn't seem to care. They grunted and hissed, and snapped at Jim and the mongooses when they had a chance, but their focus was elsewhere.

They rammed themselves against the porch, and grabbed at it with both hands, lifting.

"They're trying to break apart the trailer!" Eddie barked, seeing the danger. "They're not getting past your hexes, so they're just going to tip us over or smash us to bits!" He leveled the Remington at a man who looked totally normal, and wore a blue-green-colored jumpsuit like he was a plumber or some sort of appliance repairman. He was squatting to get his hands under the lip of the porch, trying to rip planks out directly. Eddie got a good enough look at the man to see that the name on his chest read *Bob* and that his belly writhed, and then he squeezed the trigger. Blood spattered the porch, the khaki fabric ripped open and a mass of hissing serpents sprang from Bob's belly. Bob stumbled back, arms windmilling. Eddie glanced around the yard and guessed there might be fifteen or twenty of the snake-man-monsters besieging them. "We need another way out!"

Phineas fired three quick shots, brass shells spinning out of his bolt-action rifle like rolling dice between each *bang*. "Only other door's the back!" the preacher shouted. His face was slick with sweat and his voice quavered a little. "Through the tent, past the Nehushtan and on down the hill!"

"Chingones might be on that side, too!" Mike pointed out. The bass player emptied his clip into a bearded man whose lower body was a hissing knot of snakes—the inversion of Lady Legs—and knocked him back into the sand. Gray-brown mongooses jumped onto Snake Legged Man and bit at his snapping serpentine lower body.

"Have faith!" Eddie bellowed back, and shoved more shells into the magazine. "Jim! Out the back!" he yelled at the singer, and then he jumped into the kitchenette, grabbed Phineas Irving by the shoulder, and spun the preacher around to head him in the other direction. "Lead the way!"

Overalls rammed his snake head in through the kitchenette window; Eddie pointed the Remington at the flickering tongue, as long as Eddie's forearm, and squeezed the trigger.

Boom!

Then Eddie stumbled back through the trailer, on the heels of Irving and Mike, with Jim close behind them.

A tiny hall ended in a scratched dark brown door with a flaking plastic knob. Irving pulled at the handle and the door didn't budge. "It sticks!" he exclaimed.

The trailer shook and its wood groaned.

"No time!" Eddie shouldered Mike aside, pointed the shotgun at the doorknob and *boom!* blew it to pieces. He muscled past Mike and Irving both, pushing himself first through the door.

He hopped down a cinderblock step and into the tent, leading with his weapon. There were a few benches, rough-cut and dirty. The tent was propped up on four poles and some cross-beams that connected them; one side of the white canvas sagged to the ground, but there were no snakes. An iron tube sunk into a poured puddle of concrete served like a flag stand, and stuck into it was a wooden pole. The wood looked so ancient it was almost petrified, and nailed to the top of the pole, coiled around a stubby crosspiece, was the desiccated body of a snake, six feet long and a brilliant red that managed to gleam through layers of sand and dust. Eddie could smell the antiquity.

He blinked and tried not to focus on the infernal feast he saw at the back of the tent, haggard women ladling soup from a huge cauldron into bowls that they handed to a line of equally haggard men. The soup, Eddie saw, was thick with tiny fingers and toes.

"Clear!" he shouted, and stepped forward.

The trailer shifted again, and the other three men stumbled in behind Eddie. Twitch must be outside still, Eddie thought. He hoped the fairy was okay. He'd hate to have to find a new drummer; your choices were limited when you only let damned men join.

"Get the Nehushtan!" he barked to Irving.

"I … I can't," the preacher fumbled. "I … you're a man of faith. You carry it!"

"It won't work if I hold it," Eddie growled, "trust me."

Irving turned to Mike.

"It won't work for any of us!" Eddie snapped. "You said you could make it flicker, that's better than nothing! Pick it up and let's go!"

The trailer shook again, and Eddie heard a loud *CRASH!* inside it. He imagined the porch torn to toothpicks, and Overalls and Lady Legs trampling the shag carpet.

Phineas Irving flinched, gulped, and slung the Enfield over his shoulder. He bent to pick up the Nehushtan. "I've never tried this against … against things like those," he said. "Just the little rattlers. Just keeping them out of the tent so I could preach a little."

Eddie shrugged and stepped to the tent flap. The sagebrush and sand beyond wiggled and danced with a sea of snakes, but they stopped a few feet from the canvas. Eddie locked eyes with a particularly angry-looking diamondback and hissed right back at him. "Apep can crap 'em out big," he guessed, "and he can crap 'em out small. It's still all the same shit." He hoped he was right.

"Carry the tent," Irving pleaded, and he stood up with the Nehushtan on his shoulder.

"What?"

Twitch touched ground and shifted from his falcon to his humanoid forms, looking very feminine. "They're coming around this way!" the fairy gasped, and slipped his fighting batons into his hands. His long silver hair and matching horse's tail bounced with his own edgy footwork.

"I don't know if I can do it without the tent," Irving explained. "I think I can make it work with the tent."

"Jeez," Mike said, but he jumped over to one angle of the tent and picked up the pole supporting that corner.

Eddie was tempted to shoot the preacher. "What do you mean, like it's a force field made out of tent canvas?"

Irving shrugged, trembling. "I know I can keep snakes out of the tent," he muttered. "I don't know what happens if I leave the tent."

Jim nodded to Eddie, arched his eyebrows, and positioned himself at a second tentpole.

Faith, Eddie grumbled in his head. If creation had been up to him, he'd have chosen an instrument that was less finicky. "Fine!" he snapped, and grabbed one of the sagging poles. He hoisted it up onto his left shoulder, ripping a couple of tent pegs out of the ground as he did so. Twitch grabbed the fourth, and they began to shuffle forward. "I know you can do it, Reverend Irving," he said, trying his hardest to sound encouraging. Warm and supportive was not Eddie's strong suit.

The corner of the tent flapped around Eddie, sometimes obscuring his vision and sometimes not. He was at the front of the tent, with Mike, and they walked forward towards a trembling jumble of serpents.

Idiot, he thought, this is not going to work. He tightened his grip on the Remington, made sure the shoulder strap was in place so that when he'd emptied the magazine he could drop it and pull out the Glock instead. He only had one hand to work with, now.

But the snakes hissed and pulled back. Only scant feet in front of Eddie and Mike, and drawing back in parallel to the tent's advance. They weren't afraid, Eddie realized. They weren't fleeing. They were being *forced* back.

It was *working*.

He heard the crunch of Phineas Irving's feet on the sand behind him, and then the preacher began to sing.

"Onward, Christian soldiers, marching as to war,
With the cross of Jesus, going on before."

"I'd take the cross of Jesus going on before," Mike said. The bass player grunted and sweated and looked nervous. He held the pole against his shoulder with both hands, and his M1911 in one fist. "I don't really like being in front, and I'm not crazy about having a snake at my back, either."

"Don't shoot yourself," Eddie warned the other man, and then he looked back at Phineas Irving.

Irving looked like he was praying, like he was concentrating so hard he might be in a trance. And above him, nailed to the high cross, Eddie would have sworn that the serpent was *moving*.

Eddie blinked, trying to be sure he wasn't seeing a vision of some damned soul.

The snake moved. Its red scales flashed like rubies; dust and sand shook off its flanks as it coiled around and around in a spiral on the tall pole. Eddie met Jim's gaze, bringing up the rear with a tent pole on his shoulder, and saw that the big singer had noticed it, too. They both raised their eyebrows.

"Huevos," Mike said, and Eddie whipped his head back around.

Ahead of him, blinking in and out of his vision as the edges of the tent waved up and down in the desert breeze, he saw a slope down to the van, parked on the track where they'd left it. To his left were Mike and, beyond the bass player, the edge of the trailer as they slowly coasted around it. Between the van and the trailer in Eddie's intermittent field of vision came a horde of snake-men, shambling around the trailer's shoulder and hissing in rage. Eddie raised his shotgun.

Irving sang louder:

"Christ, the royal master, leads against the foe,
Forward into battle see his banners go."

"They're back here, too!" Twitch shouted.

Eddie heard the clash of Jim's sword on something hard, and then the dull thump of Twitch's batons coming into play. He wanted to risk a look back, but he couldn't. Overalls was charging straight at him, enormous head goggling in the air like a living antenna with jaws the size of a tire clamp.

The Nehushtan wasn't keeping the monster back. Or at least, it wasn't keeping it back enough. It would be no comfort if the artifact stopped the creature from entering the tent, if it could rip Eddie to pieces while standing outside.

Boom! Eddie shot the snake-man. Overalls staggered sideways, and Lady Legs rushed up behind to fill the gap.

Bang! Bang! To his left, he heard Mike taking pot-shots, too. The tent swerved and sagged as Mike adjusted his grip, but the big guy managed to still hold his end up.

They were past the trailer now and headed down the slope. Cutting across the desert in the straightest line, Eddie's combat boots tromped down on crackling sagebrush and crunching pebbles. Mercifully, he didn't step on any snakes; the little ones, rattlers and whatever else they were, continued to wiggle back from the advancing tent.

But the big mutant buggers rushed at the men holding up the four corners.

Onward, Christian soldiers, marching as to war,
With the cross of Jesus, going on before.

Boom! Eddie fired again. A handful of the pinwheel-spinning snakeheads erupting from the gabardine skirt exploded into pulp and gore, but the others kept coming. He fired again, and again, and then Lady Legs was on top of him—

whoosh!—

something sprang past Eddie.

He slipped back and rocked on his heels, his vision flashing sideways like he was on some Six Flags Chicago rollercoaster. He saw Mike swinging his pistol like a club, hammering Many Arms in the face over and over while the hands grabbed at Mike and tried to rip away the pole. Mike was taller and kept the pole out of the monster's reach, but he was being inexorably dragged down.

Then Eddie's toes hit Overalls, who rolled on the ground, and Eddie fell. He squeezed his trigger as he fell—*click*.

He hit the sand shoulders-first, hard, and lost all his wind. Vision spinning, he tried to keep his grip on the tent pole. He could see that the white canvas overhead was sagging quickly towards him, but he pushed up, hoping against hope that Overalls wouldn't bite his head off in the meantime, and kept the tent from collapsing.

And Overalls didn't bite him. Overalls rolled out of the way, squirming to get out of the tent.

Eddie lurched to his knees, climbing the pole like a ladder. He let the shotgun down to his hip and whipped out the Glock. The tent was down and blocking his view, but he knew his friends were all behind him or to the side because the tent was still up, so he pointed the pistol at the canvas, thumbed the selective fire switch to automatic mode and squeezed off two short bursts.

The gun bucked pleasantly in his hand and punched two streaks into the white cloth. When the tent opened again in the breeze, Eddie saw what had sprung past him—

the Nehushtan, the red serpent on the cross, had joined the fray. It slithered ahead of the lurching tent, throwing wide jaws that were impossibly elastic. A huge snake, thick around as a tree trunk and with a gaping mouth at each end of its body, rose hissing to contest its right of way.

The ruby Nehushtan swallowed the human-sized snake monster in a single bite.

"Holy Moses," Eddie muttered, but he saw the path to the van opening ahead of them. "Run!" he barked, and then he remembered the tent: "I mean, jog!"

They hustled down the hill. The van was two hundred feet away, and Eddie emptied out the Glock's clip at a thing with two heads. One hundred feet, and Mike tripped over a hole in the ground, like the entrance to a prairie dog's warren. He slipped and fell to one knee, and Jim dragged him to his feet.

Fifty feet and the tent fell away. It just slipped right off the crossbeams and bounced to the ground behind them like a bride's thrown veil.

Irving stopped singing and shrieked. Eddie looked over his shoulder, afraid he'd see the preacher lying on the ground. To his relief, and prodded by Jim, the man was still running, and he still held the cross on his shoulder.

But the Nehushtan wasn't eating snakes anymore. It was slithering towards Phineas Irving like it wanted to get back on its pole. Despite all it had eaten, it was the same size as it had always been and moved quick as thinking.

Behind it, in a wall, the mutant snake-people and the rattlers rolled down the hill towards them.

"Start the car!" Eddie yelled. "Reverse!"

Mike was surprisingly fleet of foot with an army of snakes on his tail, and the big man beat Eddie to the Dodge, throwing himself into the driver's seat and gunning the engine to life. Jim grabbed the preacher by the scruff of his neck just as the rubescent serpent slithered back onto its perch and hurled the man and the artifact both into the back seat of the van. Twitch didn't waste time or risk a bottleneck, simply changing shape into his falcon self and bursting into flight over the crappy brown van.

"In!" Mike yelled. The mongooses scrambled into the van as if taking his orders.

Eddie stepped into the back seat of the van and grabbed the hand strap behind the shotgun seat. "Go!" he roared, and jammed his second clip into the Glock. Still set to automatic fire, he squeezed the trigger into the wave of descending serpent flesh, letting the snakes have it as Mike threw the Dodge into reverse and slammed backwards down the road towards town.

Rat-tat-tat-tat-tat!

Eddie dropped Many Arms in his tracks, if only for a moment, and sent Snake Legged Man lurching sideways behind brush for cover. As he ran out of ammo, Jim joined him from the back seat, firing with one of the pistols lying on the floor of the van. Phineas Irving's Enfield stayed silent, though. Eddie spared him a glance and saw that the man was shaking. He was conscious, and looked lucid, but he looked scared half to death. His mongoose guard dogs slunk around his feet in the trash that cluttered the van's floor.

They retreated from the rise, the preacher's trailer disappearing with the mob of snakes. When Mike swung the van around in a quick turn where the road was a little wider, Twitch flashed in through the open door, hitting the grease-stained seat beside Eddie in his leather-clad drummer shape.

"That was amusing," the fairy said.

"It was unexpected, that's for sure," Eddie muttered. "Hey, Irving, what happened back there?"

Irving shook his bristly blond head and shrugged. "You mean with the Nehushtan?"

"Yeah," Eddie said, feeling irritated, "I mean when the Nehushtan turned into a live snake and went and ate all the other snakes."

"That's in the Bible, too," Irving said. "I think."

"Yeah, but not the Nehushtan. That was Moses's staff when he fought the magicians of Pharaoh—unless maybe those are the same thing." Eddie looked back to be sure the pursuit was out of range, and then slammed shut the side door of the van. "Hey, what do I know? But what I mean is, did you know the Nehushtan was going to get down off its cross and start taking names?"

Irving laughed, nervous. "No. I only knew that it kept snakes out of the tent, better than my hexes."

"Maybe the big red snake will heal Adrian after all," Mike suggested, looking at Eddie in the rear view mirror. "Maybe we should go pick him up and heal him and get outta this town."

Eddie looked at Irving and saw the fear in the man's eyes. "Nah," he said. "Faith don't work that way. We gotta go get the lamia. Still, the Nehushtan will probably come in very handy." The snake was dormant again, dimly red under its furred coat of dust.

"I'm going to guess Mike will volunteer for the milking job," Twitch sparkled.

"Hey," Mike objected.

Jim reached past Eddie and pointed forward.

Eddie had been resolutely not looking ahead, afraid of what he'd see, but he looked now. There again was the frozen field of ice and the wind-gnawed heads protruded from it, groaning soundlessly and staring at Eddie.

"What?" Eddie mumbled.

"I think he means the cars," Mike said. "Look how full the lot is. It was totally empty before."

"Maybe there's a sale," Twitch chirped.

Eddie grunted. He tried to shake away the vision of ice, failed, and then tried to squint past it. The parking lot around the three-story building was full of cars. Also, ahead of them, the sun inched into late afternoon.

"I would have preferred an emptier house," Eddie said. He felt tired. His burns hurt. There were two hours left on his watch's timer. "You up for this, preacher?"

Phineas Irving shook, but he gripped the Nehushtan with both hands and nodded. "I want to help your friend," he agreed. "And I want to stop Apep."

"Load up," Eddie told them all. He reached over the shotgun seat for the ammo boxes he kept in the glove compartment.

CHAPTER SIX

E ddie knew that to everyone else, he looked like he was walking drunk. But the others couldn't see the frozen heads, and he couldn't bring himself to just walk through them. In his rational mind, he knew that the sun, dropping towards the horizon now, was still fierce, but the cool desert breeze bit into his flesh like a piranha. He shuddered under the black-eyed stares of the damned and tried to stay focused on the crumbling brick cube ahead of them, even as he stumbled from side to side through the obstacle course of frozen heads.

Jim put a hand on Eddie's shoulder and Eddie looked up, catching a quizzical look from the titan of a singer.

"Same old bullshit," Eddie lied, shaking himself. "A little worse than usual, maybe, but nothing new."

"What do you mean worse?" Mike asked.

"What is it, your job to ask all the dumb, irritating questions?" Eddie chomped at him, but then he felt guilty. "I don't know," he grumbled. "Something bad happened here, I'm guessing. Some kind of terrible sin, maybe."

Twitch laughed lightly. From someone else, it might have sounded like mockery, but it lifted Eddie's spirits a little. "Sin," the fairy giggled, "is for humans."

"Yeah, it is," Eddie agreed.

Metal shutters had been dropped over the storefront windows of the Sears. It seemed a little extravagant for a box store in the middle of nowhere, but maybe that's why the Apep worshippers had chosen it. As Eddie and the band stalked around the edges of the gravel parking lot, he saw a couple who looked like small ranchers, wearing boots, yoked shirts and blue jeans, walk in through the swinging glass doors. Eddie didn't see any guards.

That made him uncomfortable.

"How trained are your mongooses?" he asked the preacher.

Phineas Irving shrugged. "Like a dog, I guess," he said. "Not as much as that, really. They fight snakes by instinct. Fortunately, they have really good instincts."

Eddie had hoped he might be able to send the animals in as scouts somehow. "I'd give a lot for a decent wizard right now," he said, thinking of Adrian and wishing he could turn invisible.

"Sorry," Irving muttered.

"Never mind." Eddie spotted something at the side of the building. "Twitch," he told the fairy, "I'm glad you can fly." He pointed and then set out at a jog.

It wouldn't pay to forget that Overalls, Lady Legs and the other mutant snake-men were somewhere out behind them, and coming their way.

The building's shadow should have given Eddie relief from the heat as he rolled to a stop underneath a fire escape; instead, it added to his sensation that he was freezing to death. He gritted his teeth, forced himself not to shiver, and looked up. The iron ladder bolted to the side of the building as an emergency exit only ran halfway down its side, but then it had a second half on tracks, that could be unlatched and pushed down from above.

Twitch hit the top of the fire escape in falcon shape and immediately became the spiked, leather-bar-garbed drummer. He skittered down the ladder like a monkey and kicked open the latch.

"Easy!" Eddie hissed, but too late. The ladder bumped, rattled and squealed like a hinge that needed oiling, but it dropped. Jim stepped forward and caught it easily before it hit the bottom of its descent, cutting off what might otherwise have been a very loud noise.

"Thanks," Eddie said to the singer.

Jim shrugged, slid the ladder easily down to its full extension, and started climbing up.

"I'll go last," Eddie told them, and sent Irving and Mike up the ladder ahead of him. Mike climbed reasonably well, for a big guy, but Irving moved slow, humping the Nehushtan on one shoulder and the Enfield on the other as he went. Then Eddie climbed up the rungs. Halfway up, he grabbed a bit of rope that was knotted around the top rung of the sliding half and pulled it up after him, latching the ladder back into place and then joining the others on the gravel-strewn rooftop.

There were air conditioning units, a small water tower and a gas generator on the rooftop. The way inside was a door at the top of a staircase. Eddie pulled at the handle and found it locked. "Mike?" he said.

"Sure," Mike said, no problem. The bass player had grown up running in gangs and had some useful skills. "I just need a credit card."

"Credit card?" Eddie snapped. "Do you think we're here to go *shopping?*"

"*Chingón,*" Mike laughed. "I can open this door, but I need a credit card to do it." He looked around at the band. "Nobody? Nobody's got a credit card?"

The band stared back dully. Eddie shrugged. "Bad risks," he deadpanned. "I guess when Satan got my soul, he dinged my credit score, too."

Phineas Irving shoved the Nehushtan into the crook of his neck and shoulder and rummaged in his pockets. "How about this?" he asked, and held out a driver's license.

Mike took it. "It's expired," he noted. "Pennsylvania."

Irving nodded. "I'm kind of on the lam," he said, and pointed at the big red snake on his shoulder.

"Isn't everyone?" Twitch cracked wise.

"Stop reading the damn thing and open the door," Eddie said gruffly. He took the Remington in both hands and stood watch.

Up here on the rooftop, at least, he didn't see the frozen heads. Just the metal hulks of building machinery and the dusty blue sky, slowly deepening.

Click. Good as his word, Mike opened the door. "Easy," he said. Eddie wished he felt as confident as Mike sounded, and resisted looking at his watch.

"Do we have a plan?" Irving asked, as Eddie headed first into the gloom-shrouded stairwell.

"Sure," Eddie quipped. "We find the lamia. Then Mike milks it." The stairs under his boots were concrete, and he shuffled slowly, trying not to trip himself. Under a glowing green exit sign, he hit a landing and turned.

"I do?" Mike asked.

The door at the top of the stairs slammed shut, and the stairwell plunged from shadow into darkness.

"What's the matter, Mikey?" Twitch asked. "Boobs are all fine and good until you actually have to touch them?"

"Don't call me Mikey," Mike complained. He sounded like he was at the end of the line. "And don't leave me. I think I'm alone back here."

"No matter what you may say," Jim sang from somewhere behind Eddie. He sang in a whisper, but in the stairwell his voice boomed, anyway.

"I always will be true.
No matter how far away,
I'll always be with you."

Eddie chuckled. "You in love, Jim?"

"You said he was a mute," Irving squeaked.

"Nah, I said he was *cursed*," Eddie reminded the preacher. "Strictly speaking, that wasn't quite true, either. He's just trying to avoid unwanted attention."

"By singing?" Irving asked. "Like *that?*"

"Why don't you do it more often?" Mike asked. "We could have, like, conversations, instead of you just pointing and looking serious and then Eddie talking all the time."

"Do you have any idea how hard it is to have a conversation entirely by singing?" Twitch demanded.

Eddie bumped his toes into a door at the bottom of the stairs. "Hold on," he urged the others. "Slow up."

"He could make up his own words and put it to music," Mike suggested. "Kind of scat-singing. Like," and the bass player burst into sing-song, "*hey, Mike, how about you pick this lock for us?*"

"That's cheating," Eddie said. "It's just talking with pitch, and it don't count."

"Why?" Mike pushed. "I mean, if they can't hear music?"

"Who's *they?*" Irving asked.

"Uh … Satan," Mike said. "And those guys."

Eddie felt something brush against his feet. He jumped almost out of his skin, and then realized it was probably a mongoose. "Just having a pitch to it doesn't make a sound music," Eddie said. He found the door handle, and pulled. This one was locked, too.

"It doesn't?" Twitch asked.

"Rhythm section," Eddie muttered. "Mike, get up here and open this door."

"This from the world's greatest tambourine player," Mike grumbled, but down he came. There was grunting and huffing as he stepped on toes and finally tumbled down to the bottom of the steps. "I still have the card," he said.

Eddie guided him to the door's handle.

"If just pitch or rhythm was enough to block a sound from the Fallen's hearing," he pointed out, "they wouldn't hear machines working, or animal calls, or just about anything else. They'd be practically deaf. It's gotta be *music*."

"He could have code songs," Mike persisted. "Like 'Beat It' could mean 'run away'. Or he could sing 'Eye of the Tiger' to mean 'attack.'"

Eddie shook his head. "I'm gonna let you think about that one on your own, Mike, and tell me why it's a terrible idea."

"I don't understand," Irving groaned.

"You don't have to," Eddie said. "Hang on tight to the Nehushtan, and remember how it drove away those crazy-ass half-snake bastards back at your trailer."

"Got it," Mike said, and pulled open the door.

Eddie dragged Mike with him and slunk out onto the top floor of the Sears. They found themselves behind a mock-up of someone's front room, with a three-part sofa and chair set and an oval glass coffee table. The floor was dimly lit, only a few sections of its fluorescent tube lighting turned on, and no windows.

"Home sweet home," Mike sneered at the furniture and drew his pistol.

"Don't knock it," Eddie shot back. "I miss this stuff." He saw bodies stacked three deep on the couches and on the floor between them, oozing red from thousands of tiny perforation wounds. They lay in puddles of their own blood, white and drained like slaughtered chickens, but they weren't dead. They were wiggling.

He looked away.

The others filed out behind them onto the floor.

"Why is the top floor Furniture?" Mike asked. "That just means they have to bring all the floor models up two flights of stairs."

"No one impulse buys a bed," Eddie pointed out. "Or at least, anyone who throws around that kind of money doesn't shop at Sears."

Mike shrugged. "Maybe they got an elevator, anyway."

"I hear something," Twitch said. "It's rhythmic, so it must not be music."

"Does it have pitch, too?" Mike snarked.

"Ah, now you're asking really sophisticated questions, and I'm just the drummer." Twitch sprang into the air and took flight as a falcon. He flapped his silvery wings and shot across the Furniture section of the Sears, dropping into a wide double-stairwell in the center of the floor.

Jim followed, and the others trailed after the singer. At the stairwell, Jim stopped and looked down. Eddie looked with him, and saw a stack of inflated, life-sized, bowling pin-shaped clowns standing guard over a table of woodscrews. He guessed it might be the junction of Toys and Hardware.

"Of course I thought he had to be a fairy when I saw him," Irving muttered. "But thinking a thing and actually seeing it are very different." The preacher shifted the Nehushtan on his shoulder, looking very out of place in the department store. Eddie chuckled. They *all* looked out of place.

"The fairy's not your problem," he told the other man. He patted the pole, freeing a falling sift of sand from the ancient wood. "Your problem is that you are our biggest gun. When the fight breaks out, we need to get you into position and unleash the power of your weapon."

"We're not in a tent," Irving said hesitantly.

"You kidding?" Eddie gestured at the floor displays all around them. "What is Sears, what is any big box store, if not just a big tent in a bazaar? And you know that the Nehushtan can rain Hell down all over these things. You don't *think* it, you *know* it, because of what you've *seen*."

"Faith seems complicated," Mike said. "I'm glad it's not me." He shifted from foot to foot, carefully checking all the corners of the floor as they waited for Twitch to come back.

"Nothing simpler," Eddie lied. "And the good news is that we've got us a powerhouse here, a man whose faith is true and weapons grade."

Mike snorted. "Weapons grade?" He laughed. "Mierda."

"It's true," Eddie said. "For your faith to be effective against evil, it's not enough to believe in God. You have to believe in evil, too, and you have to believe that your faith will protect you."

"So ... vampires ..." Mike said slowly.

"A cross ain't enough," Eddie explained. "On the other hand, a cross in the hands of someone who believes in the cross, and believes in vampires, and believes the cross can stop the bloodsuckers ... well, sayonara, Nosferatu." He patted the Nehushtan again. "The Reverend Irving here believes in snake-mutant sons of bitches, and he knows from personal experience that the Nehushtan is an ass-kicking weapon of heavenly vengeance against them, so his faith is exactly the kind we need."

"Huh." Mike scratched himself.

"Of course, we don't want you to kill the lamia before we milk her."

"I'm not really a reverend," Irving said.

"Well, you're not a Ph.D., either, so I can't call you *doctor*." Eddie snorted. "Besides, I kind of like *reverend*." Irving looked shaky, and sounded none too confident. Eddie wanted to shore up the man's faith before they got back into the thick of it, but he didn't quite know how.

"You do it," Irving said.

"Can't."

"Why not?" The preacher tried to push the Nehushtan pole into Eddie's hands and Eddie resisted. "You saw it work just like I did. You know it works. You carry it and I'll shoot the rifle."

Eddie grabbed the pole and shoved it onto Irving's shoulder, hard. "I'm damned, don't you get it?" he hissed. "It doesn't matter how much I believe or what I've seen, I sold my soul, and I can never have the gift of faith."

Irving looked at Mike.

"Yeah," Mike said. "Me too, I think."

Phineas Irving sighed heavily.

"It ain't that bad," Eddie urged him on. "Everything I said is true. We know you've got faith, and we know what you can do with the Nehushtan."

"I choked when the tent fell off," Irving reminded him. "And suddenly it stopped working, and we were almost eaten."

"This time you won't choke," Eddie reassured him, and then he pumped the Remington. "Besides, we're here with you, and we're armed to the teeth."

"I'd still rather it was you holding the pole."

"Believe me," Eddie laughed harshly, "I'd trade places with you in a heartbeat."

"What are we going to milk the lamia into?" Mike asked. "I mean, Adrian's not here, so he can't … you know …"

"Breastfeed?" Eddie asked, grateful for the change of subject. Too much thinking wasn't going to help Phineas Irving at all. He stepped over to a display of kitchen furniture and took a green pebbled plastic pitcher off the top of a finger-smudged black table. "That'll do," he judged. "We get that much milk, we can donate the extra to Johns Hopkins or the VA."

He heard a clicking sound and looked up. Standing at the top of the stairs, dim light washing his face from the story below, Jim snapped his fingers and hissed in Eddie's direction.

"Uh-oh." Eddie rushed to join the singer of the band.

Jim pointed.

The floor of the story below was awash in snakes. They were the normal-sized ones, rattlesnakes and whatever else, but there were hundreds of them. They hissed and slithered over each other and tied themselves in knots like living pretzels, batting the inflated clowns every which way and knocking showers of woodscrews to the floor.

Eddie felt tired.

"Dammit," he sighed. "All I want to do is keep us alive until we can get to Chicago, get a little help from the hoodoo woman, and save our souls. Why's it have to be so hard?"

The snakes began to climb the stairs. No sign of the big freaky mutant ones, though. Jim braced himself and Mike came around to join them, pistol ready.

"Irving," Eddie hissed, "get over here!"

Phineas Irving stumbled around to the top of the stairs. He looked like he was in shock, and the Nehushtan on his shoulder shook. "Maybe we should shoot the snakes," he suggested.

"Maybe they ain't heard us yet," Eddie countered, "so we should try something a little more quiet."

"Even Peter sank into the water," Irving pointed out.

"Just once, though," Eddie said optimistically. "The second time out, he was gangbusters. Should we sing a hymn? It's gonna have to be soft if we do. Plus," he pointed at Jim, who stood resolutely pointing his sword at the advancing snakes, "it'll mean Jim gets to join us, and it'll make him feel included."

"I ..."

"*Onward, Christian soldiers,*" Eddie started in a whisper, "*marching as to war....*"

Irving closed his eyes and moved his lips along with the music.

Come on, Eddie thought, you can do this.

The Nehushtan began to loop and slither on its pole. Eddie crossed his fingers.

"I'm taking the safety off," Mike said. "They're close."

"You've still got the safety on?" Eddie snapped, incredulous.

The Nehushtan shook off a veil of sand and coiled like a spring. It stared at Eddie, and its black, beady eyes glittered.

"You're doing great, Reverend Irving," he told the preacher. "*Christ, the royal master, leads against the foe....*"

"*Forward into battle see his banners go!*" Jim joined in. The boom of his voice filled the Furniture section, even whispering as he was.

Eddie heard the *whoosh* of wings, the angry *hiss* of a snake and a tiny *crunch* as a serpentine skull was cracked open. Twitch the horse-tailed falcon tossed a bloodied scrap of former snake to the floor and then landed in his human shape, batons in hand.

"They're getting ready for a party down there," the fairy said. He turned and joined Jim, both of them swiping with their weapons at the slow flood of snakes. "An orgiastic one."

"Where's down there?" Mike asked. Jim and Eddie continued to sing softly, as the song reached its chorus. Eddie kept his eyes locked on the preacher's face, communicating all the faith and confidence and trust he could. Out of the corner of his eye he saw the twinkling red of the Nehushtan's scales as it shifted about, and he tried not to let himself get distracted.

Onward, Christian soldiers, marching as to war,
With the cross of Jesus, going on before.

"The basement," Twitch answered. He and Jim were hard pressed by the snakes, slapping them aside and skewering them and stomping them flat. "Kitchenware. Apparently, Apep's a domestic goddess."

Ding!

"What's that sound?" Eddie asked, and stopped singing to listen. He looked into the depths of the floor where he thought the sound had come from and saw a light appear, sliding into visibility as the door concealing it opened.

The elevator door.

"Uh oh," he muttered. Over a cluster of bookshelves and a wardrobe he saw the waving, jaw-snapping head of the mutant snake-man Overalls. He couldn't see the other monsters yet, but from the sound of many feet that Eddie heard, he knew that Overalls wasn't alone.

Then Overalls turned his head in the direction of Eddie and their eyes met, man to snake.

"Hell."

"What?" Phineas Irving gulped.

The Nehushtan froze.

CHAPTER SEVEN

Eddie hurled the pitcher at the mutants. It was a pointless gesture, except that it freed his hands for the shotgun.

Jim leaped into combat in his crazy Zorro way. In two steps he was stomping on the springy center of a little kid's bed set, grinding his heel into the eye of Fuzzikins the Slumber Bear, and then he hurtled himself upwards.

Eddie didn't wait for Jim to come down. He took three steps to the side to get a clear look at the elevator and raised the Remington.

"Believe!" he shouted, and squeezed the trigger.

Boom! He missed Overalls and shattered all the glass in the windows of an ornately scrolled but gaudy china cabinet. Shards flew in all directions.

Jim skipped like a flat rock over water across the top of a high wardrobe, coming down through the air, boot heels first, on the other side.

Bang! Bang! Eddie heard Mike start unloading behind him. He didn't see what happened with the bullets, so either Mike was missing big-time, or he was shooting at the snakes on the stairs.

Jim kicked down into the grinning human head of Many Arms, flattening the mutant's ear in a spray of blood and knocking them both sideways in opposite directions. Eddie saw that all the snake-man thugs from the Church of the Redeemer Nehushtan were here—no, not quite, since the ones the Nehushtan had actually eaten hadn't reappeared, but in the meantime, the survivors had picked up a few new friends. He also saw they looked fresh and uninjured; the limb he had seen chopped off of Many Arms was now small and stubby, but it was visibly growing back.

At least with this many of them coming, he couldn't really miss. Eddie pumped the shotgun and fired.

Jim hit the ground on his shoulders and slid on the smooth floor, like a human toboggan skidding backwards and head-first. When he rolled to his feet, he came up swinging a blue lava lamp by its cord. The singer jumped back into the fray alternating swooping strokes of the lamp and sharp, quick thrusts with his saber.

Overalls lurched at Eddie, jaws gaping open and down at Eddie's head. Eddie found the creature's persistence irritating, more than anything else. He jammed the shotgun into Overalls's maw with his left hand, muzzle against the back of its throat. The mouth clamped shut, and Eddie narrowly missed losing his arm— the monster's teeth sunk into the thick fabric of his jacket sleeve. The mutant snake-man's beady black eyes glittered and he hissed. Having his fist inside the creature's mouth made Eddie feel like one of those TV veterinarians on some PBS show, sticking his arm inside a cow to deliver its calf. He felt wet snake-slobber on his fist and a bad stink clogged his nostrils.

Eddie squeezed the trigger.

The back of Overalls's big serpentine head blew out in a shower of red blood, white bone fragments and black and yellow scales. The velocity of the slug carried the monster back with it but didn't open its jaws and, with a sharp tearing sound, Eddie's sleeve ripped right off at the shoulder.

Eddie had no time to mourn for his jacket. Snake Legged Man rushed at him, his snakes for feet hissing in protest as they were thumped against the floor. At his side came a barechested guy in a John Deere cap and corduroy pants who had a mass of snakes sprouting from his back and shoulders like wings. Eddie grabbed his Glock with his free hand, whipped it out, and started entertaining the company.

Meanwhile, Jim whirled his lava lamp like a bola, tangling it around the neck of Many Arms and jerking the snaky son of a bitch sideways and off balance. Bob the repairman grabbed for Jim, trying to drag the singer and pin him against the nest of snakes writhing on Bob's chest. Jim sidestepped and lopped off the entire bush of serpents in a single swipe—

they dropped to the floor and kept swarming.

The Nehushtan, Eddie thought. He needed the snake-on-a-stick to push some of these things back.

"Why do I not hear singing?" he barked. "*Onward, Christian soldiers!*"

"Cagado!" Mike shouted back, like that was some kind of answer.

Eddie threw a look over his shoulder in between shots and saw that the Nehushtan leaned against the railing around the stairwell, and Phineas Irving worked his Enfield rifle, slamming .30-06 bullets alternately down the stairs at the snakes or past Eddie at the mutants. Mike had stuck his M1911 back in his pants and swung a club that might have been a table leg originally. He and Twitch swiped at the snakes that raged hissing up the steps, not making any progress. They might have already been overwhelmed but for the preacher's mongooses, which bit through snakes' heads with terrible efficiency and kept a frightened circle of serpent flesh milling away from them.

"Twitch!" Eddie yelled. "Get us a way down!"

"I already have one!" the fairy howled back as Eddie turned away to pay attention to the horde that rushed him. "It involves you turning into a bird!"

Lady Legs charged, a hurricane of snakes. Eddie didn't let himself get distracted by the biting mouths, and calmly aimed for one of her knees instead. *Boom!* The 870 chewed a coconut-sized hole right through the gabardine and punched the knee out backwards. Lady Legs toppled to the ground writhing and kicking, her half-disconnected leg spinning red out like a centrifuge.

A white horse flashed in the corner of Eddie's eye.

And then John Deere piled into Eddie like a freight train.

His fists were cinder blocks, and they both connected to Eddie's jaw before Eddie really even saw them coming. Snakes bit at him and he shoved the Glock into John Deere's belly—

bang!

John Deere slipped and fell in the gore, and as he dropped, one of the snakes on his back grazed Eddie's bare arm with a fang. Cold terror lanced through Eddie's heart and he leaned into his pistol, pushing it like a knife into the mutant's belly and squeezing off several more muffled shots. John Deere flailed and shrieked, the sounds coming out of his mouth sounding more animal than human.

Jim appeared, a television in his hands. The device dragged an extension cord behind it and its screen was jagged with rolling horizontal lines of static. Eddie looked up and saw that Jim had cleared a space the length of several wounded and shuddering mutants' bodies. John Deere howled and clawed at Jim's legs, and his snakes bit harmlessly at Jim's boots as Jim raised the TV—

smash!—

and brought it down in a final hammer blow that threw sparks in all directions and obliterated John Deere's head. The barechested mutant kicked his feet in one final moment of agony then was still.

And then the silvery horse flashed past Eddie again, headed for the stairs.

It pushed a bed, its chest pressing against the high headboard.

"Go!" Eddie yelled. He switched the Glock's selective fire mechanism to *automatic* and strafed the surging crowd of mutants with everything left in his clip. It didn't last long. "Go!" he yelled again, then holstered the pistol, grabbed the Nehushtan where the preacher had laid it down and jumped onto the bed.

Mike and the not-quite-Reverend Irving stumbled in with him. Jim threw his shoulder against the headboard and then vaulted over it as the bed tipped over the stairs—

and began rattling down like a big sled.

"Five little monkeys!" Mike hollered, his teeth rattling.

It occurred to Eddie too late to wonder how high the bed's legs were—if they were too tall, he thought, they might hit a step and tip over forward. He heard and felt the squishes of snakes being run over as the bed ba-ba-ba-ba-bumped down the stairs at a trot.

Twitch whizzed over the bed and ahead of it in falcon form, wings spread wide.

"Four little monkeys!" Mike laughed.

Eddie turned to look behind them and saw Lady Legs and Many Arms and a swarm of their friends lumbering after them. Including Overalls, dammit! How many times did these things have to be killed? He raised the Remington to add a few to the score before remembering that both his guns were empty.

And the second story was coming fast.

He shoved the Nehushtan into the hands of Phineas Irving and started singing. Jim joined in:

"Onward, Christian soldiers, marching as to war!"

Eddie switched clips on his Glock and shoved shells into the Remington as fast as he could without dropping them, watching the floor rise up to meet them and praying, though he had no right to pray, that Phineas Irving would just *believe*. Clowns with fixed maniacal grins bobbed back and forth, and Eddie felt like they were mocking him. He twisted around as the stairs were coming to an end and let off three quick slugs into the ravening crowd on their heels.

"With the cross of Jesus ..." Irving's voice rose to join his and Jim's in a warble.

CRASH!

The wood of the bed splintered on impact, throwing splinters in all directions and hurling Irving out of the bed. The lanky man rolled forward into a hissing wall of snakes, clutching the Nehushtan on its pole—

and the snakes parted.

"Three little monkeys!" Mike laughed, short of breath. A bobbing clown with two buck teeth in his yawning mouth bowed low and touched foreheads with the bass player. "Mierda!"

Eddie jumped off the bed and staggered to drag Irving to his feet. *"Mierda* is right!" he yelled. "Run!"

Sheets of blood ran down the walls and Eddie's combat boots stepped on a floor of heads. Damned souls stood beneath his feet, stacked shoulder to shoulder like sardines, so tightly that they made a solid floor. The flesh on their heads was worn from treading feet all the way down, exposing cracked and oozing skulls under the tatters of hair and skin that remained.

Eddie ignored them. He jammed the muzzle of his 870 up the stairwell and squeezed off a couple of rounds, and then he half-dragged, half-kicked Phineas Irving into the Toys Department.

Mike was right on their heels. Jim jumped from the demolished bed to the banister of the stairs. Out of the corner of his eye, Eddie saw the big dark-haired man slash three times at the pell-mell mutants before leaping over a shelf of sagging plush giraffes to join them, landing on his feet light as a cat.

Twitch touched down in man-shape as they raced through a depressing junkyard of dusty fire trucks and no-name action figures, but immediately took to the air again as a falcon. Eddie saw why and pumped the shotgun. "They're bad enough when they stick to the ground," he muttered, and pulled the trigger.

Two flying snakes in the way of the Remington's slug exploded into shuddering meat. Two out of a thousand.

Phineas Irving sang louder and he sweated rivulets of salt, but he was still singing.

The wall of flying snakes hit the Nehushtan's bubble of faith— and bounced back.

"Yee ha!" Eddie shouted. "Onward, Christian soldiers!"

They rounded out the back of Toys at the top of the next flight down in a no man's land between shrink-wrapped wire crates of fake plastic food labeled to look like off-brands on one side and a pallet of two-by-fours on the other.

"Down!" Eddie barked, and pushed Irving and Mike forward, after the flashing horse's tail of the falcon Twitch.

He joined Jim at the back. The singer ducked under and wove around a hedge of snakes that snapped and hissed at him from the floor as well as from the bodies of the mutants—Lady Legs charged at him, along with Bob the repairman and others Eddie hadn't yet bothered to recognize.

Eddie squeezed the trigger of the 870, letting off several rounds into the horde and setting them back a few paces.

"Don't mind us back here!" he yelled to Irving, retreating from the serpents in a quick skipping shuffle down the stairs. "Everything's under control!"

"*Forward into battle* ..." came the indirect reply.

They hit the ground floor, and it was ice. Heads protruding from the ice surrounded Eddie, and he was close enough now that he could see the words they were mouthing.

Save us, they said, and *I'm sorry*, and *Soon you too will join us.*

Eddie turned with Jim to see the late afternoon sun through the glass doors. He saw more heads out in the parking lot, but he saw cars, too, and with half his heart, he wanted to ditch Adrian and run like the devil.

Then the snakebite he'd got from John Deere's wing-snake itched, fiercely. It stung. Eddie scratched at it, and saw that Mike and Irving were hesitating, too. "Go on!" Eddie bellowed, channeling his Inner Sergeant. "The basement, Twitch said!"

They ran through racks of brassieres and panties. Mike's choice, Eddie thought. Guy can't stop thinking about tail, even when he's getting shot at. He could hear the sound that Twitch had been talking about now. It was a chanting, with a drumming mixed in, the shaking of metal rattles. If it counted as music, he thought idly, it did so only barely. It sounded like the crap he'd played for Sharon back when she was in college and he was just back from Iraq, and he wanted to impress her with his sophisticated interest in things African.

Bullshit, he snorted now. Gimme a fuzzed-out, wailing guitar solo any day. That's the music of my people.

He forced himself to ignore the freezing heads, and charged straight through them. They flinched as he struck them, but of course he didn't feel anything. They were ghosts, figments in a vision. Still, it was strange that they seemed to see him back. By a rack of underpants printed with fading images of Space Ghost and Quick Draw McGraw they turned again, and charged down towards the basement. Eddie wasn't sure what to expect, and whatever it was he might have imagined, it wasn't what he saw.

He stopped, several steps from the bottom, and stared. The basement was thronged with people. It might have been a Kitchenwares Department once, but the shelves and tables of merchandise had all been shoved to the walls to make a great empty space in the center of the floor. In the center of the floor lay a dog on a low-end kitchen table, a charcoal barbecue grill full of smoldering incense, and two figures.

The mongooses stood beside Eddie on the steps, rearing up and hissing.

Miriam was unmistakable.

She towered above him, voluptuous and dark and naked. Eddie gulped, trying to concentrate and not be distracted by the sheer lush sexual power that oozed out of her full lips and breasts, her thin neck and large eyes. It helped that from the hips down she became a huge, blue-scaled serpent. Her human body was ordinary in size, he realized; it was the serpent half that coiled up and pushed her off the floor, made her tall and menacing and monstrous. Her hair helped bring him back to his senses, too—it was a sleepy, rustling mass of blue snakes. In her hand she held a long flake of glassy black stone over the dog, like a primitive surgeon about to cut into a patient.

Aaron was almost as easy to identify. He looked like Phineas, a tall, gaunt, blond man wearing a trench coat. Only where human hands should have protruded from the sleeves of his coat, Aaron had snakes' heads instead.

The ceiling was a sheet of ice, and white, naked bodies hung from it by their necks. A buffeting gale that Eddie could almost feel chewed at their flesh and made them sway back and forth like human wind chimes.

The two lovers stood in a central space empty but for the dog on the table. Surrounding them was a crowd, chanting words Eddie didn't recognize, beating small hand drums and playing sistra. A sistrum was a brass rattle from ancient Egypt that looked something like the hollow metal head of a hairbrush with loose rods jammed through it. Eddie knew what they were because of Bible class, way back when, and he knew what they were because they were related to the tambourine.

Damn tambourine. Should have said *guitar player.*

At the edge of the crowd, standing in four points that approximately made the four corners of a square, were totem poles. They were wooden and crude, and each had only one figure carved on it. The nearest looked like a monkey's head, and, taking them in at a glance, Eddie thought he saw a dog and a bird and a human. They looked vaguely Egyptian, or at least they looked like someone's bad imitation of Egyptian art. All of them had long strips of cloth bandaged around their eyes.

Eddie's arm really hurt, and he didn't know why.

The dog on the table whined, and only then did Eddie register what was actually going on in the scene in front of him. The dog was alive, but its ribcage was cracked open, exposing heart, lungs and other things Eddie couldn't immediately identify, in a soupy mass of blood, organs and living flesh. Ropes held the dog to the table, but it might also be sedated—it wasn't struggling. A row of stone bowls lay on the table beside the animal, and each bowl held a little puddle of meat, like sorting bowls for a butcher.

Miriam—the lamia, Eddie forced himself to call her in his mind—stooped and grabbed the heart out of the dog's chest, severing the connecting arteries with a single swift slice of her stone knife.

"Ayayayayayay!" she wailed, and in a single gulp she devoured the heart while it was still beating.

The dog's whine became a yowl, but then Aaron leaned over it, the snakes' mouths that served him for fingers snatching what must be a heart out of one of the bowls and massaging it into the cavity from which the dog had lost its natural organ. The replacement seemed to fit, and the dog still moved, though its new heart looked smaller to Eddie's eye.

It's a snake's heart, he thought. Were they replacing all the dog's natural organs with a snake's parts?

"We consecrate thee Wepwawet, opener of the ways," Aaron chanted. "Thy heart is pure in the ways of the serpent. Thy breast nourishes all his words."

The sistra exploded in a burst of noise. It wasn't chaotic, Eddie realized. There were various sections of sistrum players, and they were playing different rhythms. But all the rhythms hit a crescendo together as Aaron finished his short dedication. The swaying legs of the damned dangling from the ceiling looked perversely like dancers.

And then, over the heads of her congregants, the lamia saw the band.

"Infidels!" she shouted, pointing a long-nailed bloody finger. "Enemies of Apep! Unbelievers!"

"Huevos," Mike muttered.

Then Eddie realized that he'd been standing and staring like an idiot while Jim, behind him, kept the mutants at bay. He turned to help and saw Jim slashing at three of them, but Lady Legs and Overalls and Many Arms, hiss though they might, weren't attacking.

They hopped back and forth and raged within a cloud of flying serpents, similarly angry and similarly harmless. Jim and the mongooses picked off many of their number, but the well of enemy serpents seemed bottomless.

They were all being held back by the power of the Nehushtan, and the faith of Reverend Irving.

The preacher still mouthed hymns. He was pale and sweaty and he trembled, but he nodded slightly to acknowledge Eddie.

"Good job," Eddie patted Irving on the back and raised his shotgun, pointing at the mass of cultists in front of him.

They were a mix of ordinary human-looking folks in rural Oklahoma outfits and people with minor mutations—gifts of Apep, Irving had called them. A boy with a perfectly ordinary face stared at Eddie out of unblinking snakes' eyes. A girl near him had human eyes, but a face that was scaly and lacked nostrils around the slits of her nose. Elsewhere forked tongues slithered between human lips, and under a white cotton dress, Eddie heard the sound of a rattle. The worshippers pushed forward, but the Nehushtan held them back, too. The ones in front grimaced in pain. Eddie didn't know if they were getting pushed too hard by their friends behind them, or if the Nehushtan itself was burning them. Either way was fine with him.

He pumped the shotgun. "We don't give a rat's ass about Apep," he called over the heads of the crowd.

Phineas Irving chanted hymns at his side; the other guys in the band stood at bay, weapons out and pointed at the snake-people.

"This is a free country, and if you want to go to church with snakes, that's your own business." He tried not to cringe back from the pallid, frozen feet hanging directly in front of his face.

"What are you doing here?" Aaron Irving demanded. "You've wounded many of my people!" He didn't move from beside the mewling dog, and the sistrum players stayed in place and kept up their rhythm. What had he called the dog? Opener of the ways? That sounded like the kind of thing Adrian was always working into his incantations. This was no ordinary worship, Eddie realized. This was a magical ritual.

This was the summoning.

He felt warmer than he thought he should, and wiped a scalding dew of sweat from his brow before it dripped into his eyes. "All I need," he said slowly and deliberately, trying to radiate calm strength like he was talking to an unhappy dog, "is a few moments of cooperation from the lady. Nobody else has to get shot or bitten."

His arm hurt.

The lamia straightened until she nearly scraped the ceiling, the snakes of her hair coming to life and hissing at Eddie. "Phineas," she called in a voice husky with lust and treason, "why do you want to hurt me?"

Beside him, Eddie felt Phineas Irving collapse to the floor.

CHAPTER EIGHT

Pump and squeeze, pump and squeeze, pump and squeeze—spent cartridges chunked onto the stairs and Eddie's shotgun blasted ragged holes in the attacking crowd, but after three quick shots the Remington was ripped from his hands. Knuckles plowed his eyes and his jaw and angry fingers dragged him to the ground so boots could kick him, over and over again.

"Don't kill them!" he heard the husky voice of the lamia cry. "Apep likes his meat fresh!"

Then something stabbed Eddie in his arm, really hard, and he lost consciousness.

O O O

Eddie's hands were empty. He wanted a knife, or a roll of tape, or anything. A gun, especially. Not that it would have done him any good.

Sharon and the kids were on the ground in front of him. Not the ground, the floor. They lay on a red carpet, tied and helpless. Sharon was dressed in a suit like she'd wear to work, and seeing her made Eddie wonder for the thousandth time what on earth Sharon, a gorgeous girl with a college degree and then an aggressive and successful investment advisor, had ever seen in a guy like him. Marriage was the most important investment of her life, and she'd screwed it up. I screwed it up for her, Eddie thought. The girls were dressed for school, in modest plaid skirts, knee-high socks and maroon sweaters. All three were disheveled and battered, like they'd been run over or mugged. There was fear in their eyes.

They were afraid of Eddie.

Fire licked up the heavy curtains all around them; they were in a palace, or something that was furnished to look like one. Above him, a heavy chandelier swung uneasily on its chain, throwing shifting yellow light onto Eddie. Sweat poured down the guitar player's entire body, but it did nothing to cool him.

You want out? Rumbled a dark, heavy voice behind Eddie. Terror kept him rooted in his spot, and prevented him from looking around. He felt hot breath on the back of his neck and he smelled goat-stink. *Pay the price.*

"No," Eddie said, like he'd already said a million times. "They're innocent!"

The voice laughed. *No one is innocent*, it laughed. *Especially not them. Especially not her. Pay the price, or you're a dead man, as well as damned.*

"I'm unarmed!" Eddie roared, feeling flames crackling about his ankles.

You didn't need a weapon when you decided to kill my child, Eddie Marlowe, the voice boomed. *Use your hands. You are your own most dangerous weapon.*

"No, dammit!" Eddie yelled.

The fire engulfed them all.

O O O

Eddie opened his eyes to the sight of dangling feet and a sheet of ice. He felt weak and sluggish. "Where am I?" he muttered.

"The ass end of the universe," Mike told him. "In Nowhere, Oklahoma. At Sears. Locked in Customer Service."

"Soon to be the belly of Apep the snake-god, though," Twitch added cheerfully. "They say that a change is as good as a rest."

Eddie's arm ached and he was dripping with sweat. He sat up. His head pounded relentlessly, he was feverish, and his tongue was enormous and dry. He felt like he had a whole potato in his mouth, and the potato was covered in sand.

"What happened?" He saw that the other sleeve had been ripped off his jacket and the sturdy green cloth had been torn into strips and made into a bandage. No, not a bandage, a tourniquet—in his lean, wiry arm, Eddie saw the X-shaped cut under the tourniquet through which someone had sucked out the poison from his snake bite.

Some of the poison, anyway. Eddie felt like hell. He wondered if being a thin man was a disadvantage, where the poison was concerned. Maybe a bit of fat in his arm would have slowed the venom.

"You ain't been out long," Mike reassured him. "They locked us up is all you missed, and then we cleaned you up a bit."

Eddie realized that part of the pounding in his head came from the noise of the chanting, the drums and the sistra, which he could hear loud and clear. The Customer Service room was split in half by a counter, and Eddie was sitting on top of it. Three walls ran all the way up past a thicket of pipes to the concrete ceiling, and there was a metal grate like a garage door on a prison cell, walling off the fourth direction. The music was really, really loud. He stepped down off the counter gingerly.

"Thanks for making my sleeves match," Eddie cracked. "You know how particular I get about fashion."

The Nehushtan lay in the corner of the room, but at a quick glance Eddie could see that no one was otherwise armed. Phineas Irving crouched in a black office chair, face on his knees like a whipped dog. He had one mongoose on his lap, and the others tumbled around the wheels of the chair. They were bloodied and maybe injured, but still hyperactive. Maybe the blood all belonged to the snakes they'd killed. Twitch perched on his heels on the edge of the countertop. Mike stood and Jim paced. They all looked worse for wear, but especially Jim, who had bruises on his face and cuts on his arms; the big guy must have gone down swinging.

"They tried to break that thing," Mike said, seeing Eddie eyeing the Nehushtan. "They couldn't do it, so they threw it in with us. I don't think they liked touching it. It was like it burned them."

"So we got one weapon, anyway," Eddie muttered. "Too bad Moses didn't heal the Israelites in the wilderness by raising up a decent submachine gun." He patted his pockets and found they hadn't stripped them of any of the usual clutter. "Maybe I could duct tape them to death."

He stepped over to the chain link wall and looked through. The wall was bolted down by a thick padlock running through its bottom edge and a ring in the floor. Beyond was a short hall with men's and women's restrooms and a door marked *EMPLOYEES ONLY*. Janitor's closet, maybe. The hall ran right into the main area of the basement.

Eddie knew they were in the basement, of course. He could still see the legs of the damned dangling above him. He wondered why the vision of the field of ice, the heads sunk into it and the flesh-stripping wind was so persistent. He didn't remember anything about that in the Bible, but of course the Bible saw Hell mostly as fire. Tares were pulled up and thrown into the fire; trees that didn't bring forth good fruit went into the fire; death and Hell were cast into a lake of fire, the second death of the Revelation of St. John.

That wasn't quite how Eddie saw Hell, though. Fire would have been clean and quick and merciful, compared to what Eddie saw through his Infernal Eye. Of course, he saw more than just visions of Hell through his damned eye. He saw Infernals themselves, when they were present. Maybe that's what he was seeing here—though the people trapped in the ice field didn't look like demons.

Jamming his head into the corner between the wall and the bars, he could make out the backs of worshippers and the corner of the nearest totem pole. None of the cultists paid any attention to the short hallway at the rear, or to the prisoners in Customer Service. And why should they? Eddie's heart sank as he contemplated the poverty of his chances.

"That big tube up there runs air," Twitch said, and pointed at an accordion-like flexible conduit. Eddie saw a rip in the tube's fabric and guessed that Twitch must have already examined it in bird form, and torn open a hole. "But it would never support the weight of a man, and it's full of snakes."

Jim pointed at the mongooses at the preacher's feet.

"Yeah, but then what?" Mike asked. "Unless those mongeese ... mongoose ... mongooses, whatever ... are ninjas, too, getting them out ain't gonna help us any." He licked his lips.

"Nervous, Mike?" Eddie chuckled.

"I'm not excited about going to Hell," Mike admitted.

"You shouldn't be," Eddie grunted. "But don't give up yet." He considered. The music was thunder in a box, loud enough that he could barely hear the yelps of the vivisected dog as tiny chirps, nearly inaudible accents over the throbbing, droning wall of sound. He almost grabbed the earplugs out of his breast pocket and popped them in, like he'd do onstage, but decided he'd better risk the hearing loss.

Eddie shook his head, clearing fog out of his vision. He felt like throwing up.

"We can stop the summoning," Phineas Irving suggested. "If we can get out, anyway."

"How's that?" Eddie focused on Irving's words and clutched the bars of his prison, trying to fight through the vertigo and stay conscious. He was poisoned, he knew. He was dying.

"The columns around the circle," the preacher said. "They represent the four sons of Horus. They're present at the ceremony for the purpose of being blinded. Blinding them is a magical ward that prevents the gods from seeing the summoning of Apep, and stepping in to put a stop to it."

"Nope," said Mike, "now you're talking crazy. You're saying that the Apep worshippers summon the sons of Horus first, and then they blind them so they can't see that they're summoning the big snake second?"

"Yeah," Irving agreed, "that does sound crazy. But that's not what I'm saying." He thought carefully. "Look, don't think of it as religion, right? This isn't church. It's a magic spell. And the sorcerers don't want attention, so what they do is include in the spell an element that will hide it."

"Okay ..." Mike said slowly.

"This is all just sympathetic magic," Irving sniffed. "James George Frazer? *The Golden Bough*?"

"Nope," Mike frowned. "You're talking to the wrong guy. The guy you want got bit by a snake and is lying in a coma in a topless bar."

"Look, it's simple. Like produces like. So if you don't want the gods to see, you set up their images and you blind the images."

"Why the four sons of Horus?" Mike asked. "What about all the other gods, like … uh, Odin and Odysseus?"

"The four sons of Horus stand for the four cardinal directions," Irving said thoughtfully, "and the four seasons. They represent the whole universe."

"*All* the gods," Mike said. "I get it. So we take off their hoods and then what? The gods see and step in?"

Irving shrugged. "I don't really know. I think these things are all intricately tied together, so hopefully if we take the hoods off, it crashes the whole summoning. Or maybe, yeah, whoever it is that put Apep in his cage in the first place jumps in to keep him there. Ra the Sun God in some stories, or Bast, who had the head of a cat."

"Don't like *her*," Twitch tsked.

"See?" Eddie snarled. "I knew I should have gone into Egyptology."

"Really?" Mike asked. "'Cause what I really wish knew more about is guns and kung fu."

"What do the ancient Egyptians say," Eddie hazarded a question, feeling a little drunk, "about people frozen in a lake or a glacier, with only their heads sticking out?"

Irving frowned. "The Egyptians?" he considered. "Nothing. Isn't that Dante?"

"Dante? You mean, the *Inferno?*" That sounded a propos to Eddie.

Irving shrugged. "I'm not a lit guy, but yeah, I've read Dante. I think that's one of the circles of Hell. Uh … traitors, maybe."

"And they're ripped apart by a nasty, nasty wind?" Eddie added.

"I think that's Dante, too." Irving frowned. "Different sin though, I think. Maybe … usury?"

"Could it be lust?" Eddie suggested.

"Could be."

Eddie looked at Jim, and Jim nodded confidently. Eddie snorted. Jim ought to know; he'd lived all over Europe for a long,

long time, and probably knew Dante personally. Lust and treason, though, that made sense, for a description of a bunch of orgy-happy cultists who wanted nothing more than to betray their own kind to snakes. So what was he seeing? The souls of the mutants? Their future punishment in Hell?

"Kung fu is overrated," Eddie opined. He felt dizzy. "Stick to the guns."

Jim cleared his throat.

"We ain't here for the ritual, though," Eddie reminded the others. "We're here for the lamia milk."

"We could run," Mike suggested. "Just get out, rip off the blindfolds and run like the devil."

"And Adrian dies?" Twitch asked. He looked like a woman now, and Eddie wondered if he was getting ready to Glamour Mike into cooperation.

"No, I mean … maybe the Nehushtan can cure him. Isn't that what it did in the Bible?"

"Good point." Eddie didn't think the Nehushtan would heal Adrian, any more than he thought it would heal *him*—neither of them, he thought, was entitled to any of the gifts Heaven bestowed on men of faith. He knew the Left Hand was on him, but he was dying now anyway, and anything was worth a try.

Eddie was woozy, but he started towards the Nehushtan. Halfway across the room, he collapsed.

"Cojón," Mike commented.

Jim picked up the Nehushtan and handed it to the preacher. Gold glinted on Irving's hand, and Eddie realized that, weird as it was, the preacher must be wearing his wedding ring again.

"Believe," Eddie croaked, his face pressed into hard gray industrial carpet squares. Dragging himself up onto his elbows, he repeated himself. "Believe!" He wasn't entirely sure who he was talking to.

Irving didn't look like he believed, but he looked like he wanted to.

"Come on!" Eddie snapped. "I'm dying!"

"I believe!" Irving hissed. "I believe in God and the power of the Nehushtan, anyway, I just … I'm not sure I'm the right man."

He wrapped both his bony hands around the Nehushtan's pole and closed his eyes.

Jim stood behind the preacher and sang something, but over the ringing in his ears and the drone of the ritual, Eddie couldn't hear it. He stared into the snake eyes of the Nehushtan, begging it to get off its pole and ... something. And heal him. This couldn't be how he died, Eddie was sure of it. He had been seeing visions of his own death since that fateful night at the crossroads, and this wasn't it. His death was to come by fire, in a palace, together with his family.

That was most of the reason he'd stayed away from them—they couldn't die, none of them could die, until the moment came that Eddie always saw in his dreams, when they were all together. That was the ultimate terrible irony of Eddie's failed bargain with Hell; he had done it to provide for his family, but the result forced him out of their lives. At least for now, and maybe forever. He just couldn't risk bringing the events of his terrible repeated dream to pass, even if, stubbornly, they were inevitable.

Unless his recurring dream was a trick. Staring at the Nehushtan, Eddie started to laugh. His mouth was dry and sweat ran down his face, but the thought that he had pinned so many hopes, and lost so much time he might have spent with his family, on what might be nothing more than a lie punched him right in the cynical part of his sense of humor and once he started laughing, it was hard to stop.

After all, Old Scratch had tricked him about his gift, giving him amazing tambourine chops when he wanted to play the guitar ... why not give him false visions of death, too? Forcing Eddie away from his family for nothing struck him as just the kind of practical joke that would appeal to the head of the Infernal Council. Maybe separating him from his family was Eddie's real damnation.

"You okay?" Mike asked. "You all right, or did you go crazy?"

Irving's knuckles were white with effort and Eddie's eyes hurt from staring, but the snake remained frozen in place. Finally, Eddie collapsed forward onto the floor. His burned buttocks hurt, and his snake-bitten arm and his belly. His muscles all felt like rubber and he had the mother of all fevers. He'd never felt worse in his life.

"Yeah," he muttered into the carpet. "I ain't cured, but I'm all right."

He dragged himself to his feet with the counter, and Twitch jumped down to help.

"Mike," he said. "Have you looked at the lock?"

Mike nodded. "No big deal, just the same kind of thing you'd put on your storage locker, but I got nothing to pick it with."

Eddie dug into one of his pockets until he found a hairpin and a paperclip. He untangled the latter from a folded stick of gum. "Either one of these work?"

Mike grinned and took them both.

"Here's what we're gonna do," Eddie laid it out. "Mike picks the lock. Irving takes the snake-on-a-stick. We arm ourselves out of the janitorial supplies—hopefully that's what's across the hall, since it's probably too much to hope that the manager has a gun locker. We rush the first totem pole and rip its hood off. Then we do whatever we can to get to the lamia."

"Ah," said Twitch, "so it's a sophisticated plan."

Eddie shot him the evil eye. "You wanna bolt," he said, "now's the time. Fly on outta here and spend the rest of your long, fairy-ass life alone."

Twitch was quiet.

"Or stick with us," Eddie continued. "Next stop for this band's Chicago, where we got a little business to take care of." He straightened his jacket and cleared his throat. "We just gotta get through a minor obstacle first."

Twitch was a man again. He smiled, bowed slightly, and plucked his fighting batons from thin air.

"You need the milk, too," Irving said quietly to Eddie.

"Yeah, I do," Eddie admitted. "But it ain't lack of faith on *your* part that makes the Nehushtan not work on me. It's lack of faith on *mine*. I'm a damned man, I told you, and I can't have the gift. But *you*," he clapped the preacher woozily on the shoulder, "you've got it up the wazoo. So you're the key part of the plan, got it? Without you working the mojo of the Moses snake, we ain't gonna get to the totem pole."

"I have faith," the preacher said. He said it so confidently that Eddie almost believed him. "If we die, but we stop Apep, we won't have died in vain."

"I ain't gonna die," Eddie said, willing it to be true. "Not today. Someone promised me that once, and I'm gonna hold him to his promise, come Hell or high water. Mike?"

"Done." Mike picked himself up off the floor with the open padlock in his hand.

Eddie grabbed the chain door and hoisted, but his strength was sapped and he couldn't budge it. Jim, big pale rugby-looking lunk that he was, stuck two fingers into the gate and raised it up over his head in a single gesture.

"Damn showoff," Eddie grumbled, but he shot Jim a grateful look.

If anything, the noise of the magical ritual throbbed even louder in the hall. It was almost groovy, the complex rhythm that the sistrum players had going, though it was too complex to be easily danceable. That kind of rhythm took practice and real coordination. The *EMPLOYEES ONLY* door was locked, so Eddie stepped aside and stood guard while Mike worked his magic on it.

"We consecrate thee Wepwawet, opener of the ways," he heard Aaron's voice over the noise. "Thy brain is purified by the fire of the serpent. Thy vision is free of taint."

Idiots, Eddie thought. At least the ritual wasn't over yet. He kept an uncomfortable eye on the backs of the cultists. They danced and pressed forward, humans and mutants and actual snakes all alike, as if they were watching the concert of their lives. Like the Rolling Stones and Led Zeppelin were playing on the same tiny stage.

Hadn't Irving said that Apep was going to eat some of them? What kind of stupid religion was that?

Of course, he and his comrades were supposed to be the appetizers now. Eddie wished he had a gun.

"Open," Mike said, and stepped aside. Eddie tried to pick up a jug of cleaning fluid and a box of lye flakes, but found he couldn't heft either. He settled for a straw broom and stood aside, leaning on it, while Mike and Jim loaded up with chemicals and box cutters.

"Here we go," Eddie said softly. He looked at his watch just in time to see the countdown slip below the one-hour mark. He really hoped Adrian hadn't been too optimistic in his estimate of the time.

BOOM!

A dazzling light suddenly burst into the dim basement of the Sears, accompanied by the stink of sulfur. Eddie staggered and caught himself with his broom, then looked toward the ritual, shielding his eyes with his hand.

The sistrum players had changed rhythms, but continued, their patterns as complex as before. The worshippers at the back of the circle, nearest the band, still faced into the center, but now they were beginning to step out of their clothes. Fine, Eddie thought. Naked and disarmed was better. The incense cloud was thick in his nostrils.

In the center of the circle, beside the makeshift surgical table, there was a hole in the air. It looked like a streak of starlight had been painted onto nothing at all, or an invisible curtain had parted and directly behind it was a lighthouse, blazing at full power. Eddie blinked against the strength of the light and tried to keep his attention on the figures in the middle.

With a final slash of the stone flake knife, Miriam the lamia freed the dog from the ropes that still tied it to the table. Eddie saw that its chest was stitched shut now, but of course, the dog couldn't possibly be alive, not after all its organs had been replaced.

But as he watched, the dog—Wepwawet, opener of the ways?—rolled over. It rose quite steadily onto all fours, sniffed at the air and jumped to the ground.

And then padded forward quickly, disappearing into the blazing gap of light.

CHAPTER NINE

No!" Phineas Irving yelled.

Eddie wanted to punch the preacher in the face. The cultists nearest the band stopped in the last stages of their disrobing and turned to see the source of the noise. A bald man, with sagging flesh, wiry gray curls of hair all over his body and ridges on his skull like a lizard, met Eddie's gaze and hissed in disapproval, showing a row of needle-like teeth and a preternaturally thin tongue.

"Screw you," Eddie muttered, and jammed the end of his broom into Ridge Head's eye. The fat man jerked back from the blow and doubled over in pain.

Something orange flashed past Eddie and spun out over the crowd. It was a box, Eddie saw, like a large box that baking soda might come in, and it shed big white snowflakes as it flew. From the shrieks that erupted from those that were hit, he guessed that the flakes were lye. The worshippers clawed at their faces and cringed and Jim launched into them like a vengeful comet, box-cutter spinning without mercy.

"Sing!" Eddie shouted. "Or pray, or whatever!"

Ridge Head lurched forward, grabbing with both hands for Eddie's throat. He felt weak, but he managed to stumble under the attack and avoid it, probably because Ridge Head's face and eyes were already red from the lye and the broom handle, and he was blinking out too many tears to see straight. The lizard-man's nudity and blindness made his testicles an easy target, and Eddie launched a knife-hand of knuckles into the soft tissue, twisting and tearing and dropping the mutant to the floor in a spray of blood and shrieking.

Twitch whizzed past on Jim's heels in falcon shape, and then Mike lumbered by. Eddie saw that the singer was already bogged down in fighting the crowd. He pushed off one man's shoulders to springboard with his boot heels into another's chest; he grabbed a snake-legged woman by the hair and cracked her forehead-first into the nose of a heavy bearded man with snakes' heads dangling limply from his clavicle; he sliced with the box cutter, eviscerating in a single blow two men rushing him with knives; he grabbed a snake-headed freak by the ankles and hurled his feet toward the ceiling, dropping the monster onto its face on the floor. But there were just too many of them. They grabbed Jim by the elbows and shoulders and pulled him back, swinging and kicking, to the ground.

Mike threw a gallon jug of something orange on a knot of them and they hollered and hissed in protest. A second gallon, colorless, smashed into their faces as they looked up, and then the big bass player plowed into them, bellowing like a bull and cursing like a Mexican pimp.

They were both still several rows back behind the sistrum players. In the center of the room, worshippers rushed forward into a thickening cloud of incense. Without being able to pay much attention to it—and sure as hell without *wanting* to—Eddie noticed that the surgery table had become an altar-bed. Phineas's snake-armed brother, naked now, savaged one prone woman with his hips while others rushed to embrace and caress the coiling monstrosities that sprouted from his shoulders. The lamia Miriam rose beside the shimmering gate of light, singing, while men and women alike pressed themselves to her sides, stroking her body with their hands and mouths. Most of the snake-snakes and the winged snakes in the room clustered around the table and the lamia, pressing to get into the action like so many detached, living organs. In their frenzy, they pushed each other against the incense brazier-charcoal grill, and the stink of their scorched flesh added a new note to the reek of the ritual chamber.

Above them all, the legs of the frozen damned twitched and shook in a frenzy of restrained motion.

"This is just wrong," Eddie grimaced, and limped forward into the fray.

"Onward Christian soldiers," he heard Phineas Irving trying to sing behind him, but the preacher was timid and quiet, and then he faltered.

"Come on!" Eddie barked. "Louder!" He grabbed Irving by the lapel of his jacket and stumbled forward into the crowd. He looked up at the Nehushtan to see if Irving was having any success.

The snake stayed coiled on its pole. It looked still and dead.

Ahead, Twitch landed on top of the nearest totem pole. The fairy shifted from falcon into human form as he touched down, and squatted on all fours above a big carved monkey's head. Baboon, maybe. In his leather-and-spikes outfit, Eddie thought, Twitch fit right in with this crowd. He crouched low and reached down with his hands, trying to get at the blindfold over the monkey's eyes.

Three young women had Mike knocked to the ground and stood over the bass player, scratching at him with their long nails. Mike wore his cracked old brown leather jacket and it protected his arms and chest, but there were bloody furrows on his neck and the backs of his hands. He held his box cutter, but he wasn't fighting back very effectively, just raising his arms and cringing.

Mike was not the right guy to bring to a fight against naked women. He had plenty of hate and fear in him, but it wasn't directed at women. For women, what he mostly had was a slack jaw and a dumb grin.

But Eddie had enough bitterness in his heart for both of them. He swung his broom as hard as he could like a bo staff, cracking it against the temple of the nearest girl. She stumbled away, shrieking in outrage and grabbing her head. Eddie continued his charge and rammed with his shoulder into the second young woman's side. She fell squirming and breathless.

Phineas Irving stabbed the butt end of the Nehushtan's pole between the shoulder blades of the third.

"Aaaaaararaaaaagh!" she shrieked, a piercing cry that cut through the drums and the chanting. Her skin where the pole touched her charred instantly to black, like a Satanic cattle branding, and the stink of scorching flesh filled Eddie's nostrils, overpowering even the billowing incense. She crumpled to the ground and Mike staggered to his feet, just in time to meet a slithering charge from the mutant Many Arms.

This guy, Mike had no trouble attacking. Head down, he rammed the fingers of one hand into the mutant's throat while he slashed with his janitorial knife at the thing's long, scaly and exposed chest.

"It works!" Irving laughed. "It's working again!" He raised the pole like a spear and jabbed over Mike's shoulder, poking Many Arms in his human face with the butt of the pole. The mutant roared with rage and slithered back, bleeding from the cuts Mike inflicted on him and slapping at a charred mark on his face the size of a silver dollar.

Jim was back on his feet too, and crashed through a writhing pile of sex-inflamed worshippers, scattering them right and left and almost forcing open a path to the center of the circle. Eddie looked into the light—no sign of the dog's return yet, or of any giant snake. Any *more* giant snakes, anyway.

"Twitch!" he yelled.

The fairy lay on the totem pole's head on his belly, booted feet and tail hanging over one side while his arms dangled over the other. "I'm working on it!" he shouted back.

A small cloud of winged serpents rushed towards Twitch from the focal center of the orgy. "Faster!" Eddie called, and he swung his broom, smacking serpents left and right. He sucked in the sex-reeking, serpent-fouled air, wishing it were colder and cleaner and willing his head to stop spinning.

He heard the hiss of a snake at his ankle level. He spun to face it, fearing he was too late and that he was about to take a second dose of venom, but gray-brown fur flashed between him and the snake and then the snake collapsed, headless.

The mongoose kept moving, bounding off between the wrestling bodies in search of more prey. Its fellows raced around the melee with coordination, striking down serpents by the charcoal grill, around the totem poles, on the stairs, under the altar, and even low in the air.

"Got it!" Twitch yelled triumphantly. He hooked two of his unnaturally long, slender fingers into the rough cloth of the blindfold and ripped it away. Eddie held his breath.

But nothing happened. Underneath the blindfold, Eddie saw that the monkey's head didn't have eyes, anyway. It had had them once, big and bulbous, but they'd been hacked into splinters, as if by hatchets, and then burned by fire. The Apep worshippers weren't going to take any chances.

"Rats."

Eddie knocked another flying serpent away, staggered and almost fell.

Stay focused, he told himself. Get to the lamia.

He looked into the center of the rite again. Still no dog. Snakes swarmed all over the frenzied multi-participant coupling on the table, and on the swaying mass of the lamia's body. There were lizards too, he now saw, things the size of iguanas and bigger, nastier monsters, like the thing he'd battled back in the diner kitchen … that seemed a decade ago now. Worshippers of every kind pressed themselves against the lamia like piglets against a sow, writhing and squirming with ripe urgency.

Could he just slip in there with them and … feed?

The thought made him feel sick. Miriam was voluptuous, but there was an unhealthy tinge to her skin, and the snakes in her hair and her lower half made her a monstrous thing. She was blue, dammit, and more than half a snake! Some men would have been aroused—some men clearly *were* aroused—but the naked Eros of the lamia's body just made Eddie think of Sharon and curse his luck even more.

And he had to get milk for Adrian, he reminded himself. This wasn't sex, this was grocery shopping.

Besides, he'd never get in there, not with all the worshippers pressing around, not unnoticed. And he wouldn't be able to collect milk casually in a container without being spotted. He had to stop the ritual, somehow immobilize the lamia.

He just didn't see how.

"Come on." He shanghaied Phineas Irving, pulling the preacher away from a four-person pile-up that now stank of burned flesh as well as of lust and viscous body fluids, dragging the rangy man with him towards the center of the room. Where were his guns, anyway? He wondered, his vision slipping like an old filmstrip on a jerky projector. He'd give a lot right now for his pump-action, twelve gauge Remington 870 Express Magnum shotgun, fully loaded with three-inch shells.

He'd give even more for a fifty caliber M2, a pile of sandbags and a high vantage point to shoot from. Clean out this nest of snakes in thirty seconds.

Jim had opened a path through into the center of the room. He held the box cutter in his left hand now and fought with a long hunting knife in his right—he must have taken it from one of the cultists while Eddie wasn't watching. Overalls lunged at him, snapping and biting, and Lady Legs charged from another direction—

and from a third came John Deere. The man's head was still gone, a ragged bloody stump of a neck sprouting from his shoulders, but the snakes waggling from his back seemed longer and angrier, and he held a long metal pipe in his hand like a club. At least he didn't have a TV on his shoulders, Eddie thought, and then he wondered why he thought that would be any worse.

Jim fought like a dancer, weaving in and out, feinting, dodging, stepping under. The mutants tangled with each other, missing, and chased him in circles. But they were getting closer, and Jim had nowhere to go. The smaller serpents, ground-stuck and flying ones as well, began to close in on him too. The mongooses wreaked havoc among serpentkind, but they were slowing down. If they weren't injured, they had to at least be exhausted.

Eddie dragged the preacher out into the circle. "*Onward, Christian soldiers, marching as to war....*"

"*With the cross of Jesus going on before,*" Jim joined in. The guy had serious lungs on him, to be able to sing and fight at the same time.

Eddie spun with his broomstick club, knocking aside serpents, and then Twitch flashed through the central circle in falcon form, snatching two more flying snakes out of the air. Mike backed into the circle, too, his box cutter in his hands slashing half-heartedly to fend off the bare-fisted advances of two women. One had a perfectly formed womanly body but a snake's scales on her cheeks and forehead, and the other had a fine, clean young woman's face but snakes erupting from her chest instead of breasts.

Mike circled back to keep out of both their reach, but mostly he stabbed at the latter.

The sistrum players changed rhythm suddenly.

"O Wepwawet!" Aaron Irving's voice boomed suddenly from beneath a shuddering pile of women and snakes. "Wepwawet returns! The opener of the ways, behold, he comes!"

Eddie really wished he had guns.

Christ the royal master leaders against the foe,
Forward into battle see his banners go.

Overalls and Lady Legs and the others hesitated at the fringe of the Nehushtan's bubble, but Phineas Irving's voice sounded like it was losing some of its intensity.

Eddie looked around for anything else at hand that he could use—a gun, a knife, a torch, a charm, anything that might be more effective than a broomstick.

Nothing.

A dim outline began to take shape in the light of the pulsating rift. Eddie saw that the sistrum players nearest to him were just outside the space cleared by the Nehushtan. He staggered towards them, a plan spinning into being in his feverish brain. It was half-baked and half-assed and wholly insane, but what was the point of being the world's best tambourine player if he never used his chops?

Lady Legs rushed at him hissing—

and the sparkling red Nehushtan sprang from its perch, intercepting the hedge of woman-legged snakes and snapping it into its gullet in a single bite.

"No!" bellowed Aaron Irving. He sat up on his altar-bed, scattering scaly nymphlets and ecstatically hissing serpents with his sudden movement. The Nehushtan struck again, devouring John Deere whole. Freed of some of his assailants, Jim leaped spinning through the air, crashing into one of the totem poles and knocking it flying.

Eddie squinted at the pillar of light, fearing it was about to disgorge Apep himself, but the shadowy shape coalesced into a discrete form and emerged. It was the mummy-dog, Wepwawet, and it padded out calmly, looking totally normal apart from beady black eyes and a long snake-like tongue wagging from between its jaws.

And what would happen if Apep himself came out? Could the Nehushtan swallow the Egyptian god whole like it swallowed his minions? Somehow, Eddie doubted it.

Eddie shuffled and kicked his way into the row of sistrum players and snatched sistra away from them. As he plucked the instruments from their grip, some of the players kept playing, shaking their empty hands intently as if they were still making sound. Others stared at where the instruments had been in surprise.

He wondered if they were in trances. Or ensorcelled. Or high, although people who were stoned shouldn't be able to make such a complicated, coordinated sound together. Or maybe there were just enough of them playing together that they were individually trapped in the collective groove.

He thought he'd grab all the instruments and silence them, but there were too many of them, and then the rest of the worshippers lunged his way. He looked over his shoulder for help, but the others were distracted with their own problems.

Aaron Irving was standing, snake arms raised high and chanting as nude women crouched around his feet like feral cats. His brother faced off against him, staggering forward one step at a time like the Nehushtan was a boulder and he had to push it.

Eddie grabbed a handful of the instruments and retreated. Whatever it was that drove the sistrum players, he hoped they still had free will. He hoped they could see and hear, and be distracted.

Eddie, who was as good as stoned on snake venom, shouldn't by rights be able to play anything at all. The crowd loomed huge around him, naked and sweating and full of breasts and totem poles, and the room spun. But he was the world's best tambourine player, dammit. The world's *best*.

He jammed a sistrum handle into the top of each combat boot. He pinned a handle in the crook of each elbow by bringing his fists up to his shoulders, and he held two more in his two hands.

And he started to dance.

Not that he was much of a dancer, not in any formal kind of way. Sharon had paid for lessons once and he'd gone; the Foxtrot he'd been able to handle, and the Waltz, and even the Rumba, which was just the Waltz in four-four with a bit of Latin booty-shaking mixed in, but that was his limit. When he'd tried the Tango, he'd literally fallen down. Eddie didn't dance, he led the dancing from the stage.

But this wasn't a dance, not really. The sistrum was just a funky old tambourine, shaped like a hairbrush. Loaded up with six sistra, Eddie wasn't dancing—he was putting on the world's first one-man-six-tambourine performance.

He skipped in front of the section of sistrum players in front of him, trying to distract them. He needed to be the Pied Piper of Tambourines now, the most fascinating thing a sistrum player could ever see, and accidentally follow. He built up a rhythm in layers, and he built it up fast. He moved on his left foot in a slow hop, with his right shuffling and slamming down in a syncopated, ankle-twisting rattle quickly after every other front beat. He swung his left arm in slow circles, getting a steady *chink-chink-chink* out of the elbow rattle and shifting, ever-so-slightly-out-of-sync rasp on the back beats with the sistrum in his left hand. It looked sort of like a cross between St. Vitus' Dance and the Funky Chicken.

And with his right arm, he really went to town. His right elbow played sixteenth notes in an almost study drumming, deliberately omitting the third, the seventh, the eleventh and the thirteenth in every measure. The right hand played the rhythm of the melody to the song that he could hear Jim and Phineas Irving and even Mike now still singing.

"Onward Christian soldiers, marching as to war,
With the cross of Jesus going on before."

Eddie didn't need the sistrum players to follow his lead; he just needed to put on a wild enough show that it would snap them out of their pattern. Hopefully Irving was right, and the whole summoning was bound together in a tight interlocking pattern so that Eddie could put a stop to it by throwing off the rhythm.

Some of the players faltered, staring curiously at him. Eddie looked around the chamber. His friends sang and fought around the Nehushtan pole in Reverend Irving's hands in the circle. Snake mutants and flying vipers and ordinary rattlesnakes threw themselves against Eddie's friends and were thrown back by the ancient Israelite artifact, or chopped down with box cutters and cleaning supplies, or trampled by the hooves of the fairy, who now fought in his silver horse form. The ruby serpent itself was off its pole and inflicting terrible damage on the cultists, snapping up snakes and worshippers and mutant snake-worshippers with equal relish, and looking unstoppable.

Jim and Twitch and Mike, though, looked tired.

And Eddie felt exhausted. He was drained and sick, and only the Satanic power of his curse-begotten prowess with the tambourine kept him going. The sistrum players near him faltered and slowed, puzzled. They stared at him and some of them fell silent, but the overwhelming rhythm of drums and sistra and chanting continued, driven by the dozens of worshippers who didn't join in the combat. The racket was now supplemented by the squelching and grunting sounds of the further dozens who neither made music nor entered the fray, but piled upon each other in frantic animal lust all around the periphery of the room.

The chasm of light still shone in the middle of the room, and between it and the charcoal grill full of incense Aaron stood and chanted something Eddie didn't understand.

The lamia, Miriam, moved forward, shedding her more insensate micro-lovers as she went, sliding across the floor to intercept the Nehushtan.

"He comes!" Aaron Irving roared. "Behold, Apep comes!"

The mummy-dog sat obediently by the snake-armed sorcerer's side. Aaron flung his serpent arms wide like a carnival barker, and Eddie saw that something dark and very, very tall was inside the rent space full of light.

Eddie worked faster.

He hopped forward to the next bank of sistrum players. He didn't know what else to do—he had no gun, no wizard, and almost no hope. He clung to the recurring nightmare of his death, telling himself that he couldn't possibly die in the basement of a Sears in Oklahoma today, because his wife and daughters weren't here, there was no chandelier, no carpet, no curtains, no fire, no palace.

Unless that was all a lie.

The Nehushtan moved like a thing with intelligence, like it was reading Eddie's mind and trying to help him. It cleared his path, swallowing John Deere and a woman swinging a hatchet without slowing down.

Jim rushed Aaron Irving, with Mike and Twitch behind him, but a wall of snakes forced them back.

Eddie looked at Phineas Irving and saw that the preacher had dropped the Nehushtan pole. He stared at the column of light and backed away from it and snakes began to swarm in his direction.

The Nehushtan stopped, turned, and slid back towards its fallen perch.

"Oh no," Eddie muttered. He found the bank of sistrum players and shook his booty for them, knowing in his heart it was over. "Run!" he yelled feebly to the others. He was a dead man, and so was Adrian, but the others might still escape. "Run!" He knew they couldn't hear him.

"He comes!" Aaron Irving shouted again.

In his normal sight, Eddie still saw a moving shadow within the light. The shadow was immense. With his Infernal Eye, he saw a towering giant man with the head of a cobra, wearing sandals and a kilt and holding a curved scimitar in each hand.

Then another shadow rose over him, and he realized it was Miriam, bearing upon him to crush him with the coils of her body. She still held the obsidian knife, raised high overhead like she would follow the crushing body blow with a slashing attack.

"No!"

The shout was in the voice of Phineas Irving, and then the preacher slammed into Eddie, knocking him out of the way.

The lamia came down hard, square on the body of her estranged husband, with a sickening crack.

Eddie stumbled and fell to his knees, nauseated and burning, directly in front of the gate of light.

CHAPTER TEN

Nooooooooo!"

The lamia pulled back, bucking and rearing and scattering her lustful worshippers like a suddenly-charging rhino might scatter the birds feeding off its back. Lizards and snakes and snake-people staggered away in all directions.

Eddie shook himself, cracked an eye in the direction of Phineas Irving, and saw that the man was dead. Not just dead, totally squashed into a stain. His legs still existed, and one of his arms, and part of his head; the rest was a puddle of meat-pulp and blood.

But on the hand of the arm that hadn't been totally flattened, Eddie saw Irving's wedding ring.

Miriam saw it, too. She stopped for several long seconds, staring down at the bloody band of gold.

"Nooooooo!" she howled again and spun around.

Her tail was the thickness of a horse's chest where it joined her woman-shaped hips and tapered out maybe twenty long feet, covered in bluish scales. It was smooth except, Eddie now saw, twisted little fins of flesh near the end. The fins looked like bits that had once been legs and were in the long, slow process of withering away or being absorbed into the snake-flesh.

As she spun, the lamia thrashed her tail through a bank of sistrum players, killing them, knocking them out, knocking them over, and totally silencing their rhythm. The totem pole with the dog's head toppled too, falling into a writhing knot of naked worshippers with a wet cracking of bone. There had been mongooses in and around that writhing knot, Eddie thought dimly, and he wondered if the creatures had escaped.

He turned back to the gate of light, hoping it would now slam shut. It didn't. Either the ritual was a lot more tamper-resistant than Phineas Irving had imagined, or it had gone beyond the point of no return before Eddie and his friends intervened. The shadow, and the serpent-headed Infernal, loomed large in the brilliance. Lying directly in front of the gate, Eddie smelled sulfur and snake.

"Stop!" Aaron Irving cried. He stood naked before the charcoal grill, snake arms flailing. Incense billowed around him a cloud like he was being fumigated.

"We agreed!" the lamia howled. Her tail flicked right past Eddie in a blow that surely would have crushed him into jelly if it had hit him.

"It was his choice!" Aaron shouted to her. "We spared him once! He should have left us alone!"

Eddie saw Jim sweeping snakes off Mike's body with a broom, and dragging the bass player to his feet. Twitch, in his falcon form, snatched serpents from the air around the big singer's head.

Miriam darted forward and snatched her priest-lover by the throat. Their torsos were the same size, but her tail made her loom over him, and she evidently had superhuman strength, because she hoisted the man off the floor with one arm.

"*We* should have left *him* alone!" she hissed in a voice of a thousand rattles.

Eddie staggered to his feet. The worshippers were scattering, so he had a clear run at the lamia, but nothing to do once he got there. He patted his jacket pockets for something to hold lamia milk in and found the plastic cup full of jacks. That at least was something.

"He's not the first to die and he won't be the last!" the sorcerer hissed. "Besides, *you* killed him, not I!"

The lamia emitted a long, drawn-out wail, like a police siren. The chanting, the drums and the sistra were falling silent here and there around the room as the players fell victim to the spreading chaos, but Miriam's howl was louder than the musicians had ever been, and more piercing. And sad.

The gate of light stayed open.

"I killed him!" she shrieked, and then Eddie saw the back of the hand in which she held the obsidian knife.

And saw that she was wearing a wedding ring, too.

"Eternal life!" Aaron Irving choked out around the long-nailed fingers on his throat. His feet kicked helplessly off the ground and he was starting to change color to a deep purple. "Have you forgotten?"

The lamia raised him over her head and slammed him down on the table, hard. He groaned.

The mummy-dog Wepwawet barked at her and snarled. Without so much as a look of disdain, Miriam snapped her tail and threw the creature across the room. It sailed over the heads of scattering, confused orgy-goers and hit the stairs. Its body burst at the stitches on impact, scattering blood and a macabre collection of tiny organs on the concrete.

"*Love!*" the lamia shouted back at her consort, all the snakes in her hair mad and dancing with aggression. "Have *you* forgotten?"

Aaron Irving attacked her. Lying prone on his back, his snake-mouthed arms bit her flank and her neck, teeth sinking into her flesh. She didn't flinch, though blood ran down her chest and over her scales onto the floor, and sank the obsidian knife into Aaron's belly.

The priest-sorcerer arched his back, spitting blood from his mouth and nostrils. His snake arms bit Miriam again and again, on her arms, on her face, on her belly. His legs thrashed, the frantic activity of his body hurling blood in all directions. "Too late!" he shouted wetly. "He comes!"

With a last slash of the stone knife, Miriam chopped off the sorcerer's head. It bounced to the floor with a wet thud—

she swayed, lurching this way and that—

and crashed to the floor.

"Eddie!" Mike yelled, pointing at the gate.

Eddie looked down at the flattened body of the Reverend Irving. *If we die*, the preacher had said, *but we stop Apep, we won't have died in vain.*

"Hell."

Eddie grabbed the stone knife from the lamia's relaxing fingers; at least that was some kind of weapon. He blinked sweat from his eyes, stepped over her twitching tail—

and walked into the gate of light.

The basement of the Sears and the cleared-out Kitchenwares Department disappeared. The totem poles were gone, the sistrum players, the drums, the serpents, the fallen Nehushtan, the flattened Egyptologist, the altar, the dying lamia, Eddie's friends, all of it, disappeared in the blink of an eye.

Eddie still felt like total shit. His body burned and trembled and he sweated.

He stood in a long hall. It descended smoothly before him in a ramp, the floor of which felt like stone and was covered with sand. The air was warm and close and stank of snake. The ceiling of the hall disappeared in darkness, and the walls were ribbed with stone columns, with flickering oil lamps set into the stone between each pair. He heard a low humming sound, like a far-away engine idling.

He couldn't see the bottom of the passage. Below and ahead of him, he saw Apep. With his Infernal Eye, Eddie again saw the gigantic man with the head of a serpent. Apep wore an Egyptian-style headdress and simple white kilt, he had sandals on his feet, and he held a curved sword in each hand. And he was massive—maybe fifty feet tall, though the darkness and the distance might be deceptive.

Through his normal human eyes, Eddie saw an enormous cobra, hood flared—

headed his way.

The flake of sharpened stone in his hand now seemed totally inadequate. He really wished he had a decent gun. Or hand grenades.

No, he needed another kind of solution. What had Irving said? Sympathetic magic, like produces like. He was inside the ritual now, inside the summoning spell. He needed to do something to stop it, like producing like.

He realized that, out of reflex, he was patting his pockets. What did he have? The usual stuff. No hand grenades, sadly. His fingers found the plastic cup with the game of jacks in it. He'd bought the game at a gas station because the girls had liked jacks when they were younger, playing it on the stoop of the apartment building when they were supposed to be doing homework, and it had given him something to stare at and reminisce.

He pulled out the cup and ripped the top off. Could this possibly work? Or was this more insane than his Funky Chickenesque six-part sistrum performance?

Only one way to find out.

Eddie hurled the jacks down the passageway in a single handful, and the little red rubber ball with them. Some kind of incantation seemed appropriate, too, since that's what Adrian always did, only Eddie didn't know any magic words.

"Piss off, Apep!" he shouted. "Go back to where you came from! You ain't welcome anymore!"

It wasn't poetry, but it would have to do.

Apep stumbled. The giant stepped on the first of the spiky little metal jacks and winced in pain, tripping and crashing against the wall. He landed on his knee, one shoulder against a column, and stared up the hall at Eddie.

Who are you, mortal? he bellowed.

Oops.

The enormous, echoing voice sounded oddly familiar, and Eddie pegged the familiarity immediately—Apep sounded just a little bit like Jim. The thought of what that might mean made Eddie's skin crawl.

Eddie carefully put the cup and its lid back into his pocket. He planned to get out again, which meant he planned to need the cup. He didn't dare look behind him to see whether the hallway had an exit, and what it might look like.

Apep rose slowly to his feet again. *I will eat you first!* he roared, and started moving forward again, taking careful steps and watching the floor for more jack-caltrops. *I will eat you all!*

Eddie needed something else. Flashlight, pocketknife, compass, cigarette lighter, he couldn't imagine how any of it would help him. Then he grabbed the duct tape.

"Oh yeah," he said to himself.

Like produced like. Eddie fastened the end of the duct tape to the column to his left and quickly ran it across the passageway to the opposite column, where he tore off the strip and anchored it.

"I bar the way to thee, Apep," he intoned, doing his best dramatic spellcaster voice. The *thee* was a nice touch, he thought. Sharon would have been impressed, or at least she would have pretended to be impressed. Adrian would have mocked him.

No! Apep lurched forward, raising a scimitar in objection, but his feet came down on more jacks, and the giant fell to his knees, roaring.

That seemed like a good sign. Eddie ran across a second strip, cross the first at an angle. "I forbid thee passage!" he added.

Apep scrambled forward on gigantic hands and knees. Eddie could see the giant's blood smeared on the sandy stone floor of the tunnel. The swords flashed in the lantern light like a terrible two-tusked death machine, getting closer.

He ran a third strip across. Third time's the charm, he thought, and he ran it at a contrary angle to the second, so that the three strips of duct tape met in the center of the passageway like a big asterisk. A lucky star, Eddie said to himself, feeling a little panicky as the giant crashed towards him. Star light, star bright.

He wedged the stone knife into the tape for good measure, right into the center, turned so that its sharp edge faced down the passage towards the onrushing demon.

"I place this blade against thy heart, O Apep," he chanted, feeling himself getting a little carried away in the theater of the moment. "Thou shalt not pass."

Then he turned to look for a way out. Behind him rose a solid stone wall with a painting of an open doorway on it. To one side of the painted door image, to his shock, was a painting of Aaron Irving, the snake-armed man, and on the other was a picture of the lamia, Miriam. All the images were painted in what Eddie would have called, without any expertise whatsoever, ancient Egyptian style—they looked flat, with their shoulders both pointed to Eddie and their feet (Miriam's tail) all pointing inward at the door. They were dressed in what he thought of as Pharaoh-garb, too: cobra-crowns on their foreheads, kilt and sandals for Aaron, lots of eye make-up for them both.

It was troubling to Eddie to see his foes represented in tomb art. What did that mean? Was he in some real Egyptian tomb, where paintings of Aaron and Miriam showed Apep the way to escape? Was he in some magic dream-space, created only by the ritual?

But what troubled Eddie even more was the fact that the doorway was only a painting.

Wait! Apep thundered. *We can make a bargain!*

Eddie looked back and saw the snake-headed giant crouching in the hall above him. He was in easy reach of Eddie with his enormous swords now, but he stayed back, squatted in the hall with blood on his knuckles and running down his knees. In snake form he swayed from side to side, his hood flared wide and his fangs bared.

"Oh, hell no," Eddie shot back. "You got nothing I want."

He hoped.

Like produces like. Eddie turned and fell against the painted doorway, his strength gone—

No! Apep bellowed, shaking the tunnel so hard that sand fell from the ceiling onto Eddie's head and neck—

and then Eddie was through the doorway, collapsing to the ground in the basement of the Sears. Light shone on him and past him from behind, but even as he fell through, he could feel that he was being pushed, that the gate was closing shut behind him.

BOOM!

And then the light was gone, and he smelled snake and incense and saw by the blue-gray light of fluorescent tubes. At first, he just saw smears of blood on the concrete floor against which his face was pressed.

"Eddie!"

He lifted his head enough to see boots and shoes splattering through the gore in his direction. Sand fell off him as he moved, dusting the blood with an improbable yellow. His body trembled and he tried to point at the lamia, where she lay on her side next to the table, on a pile of the bodies of her worshippers and minions. "You might need to hold her down," he mumbled, and started crawling.

Jim picked him up and carried him, and Eddie saw that Jim's sword was belted around his waist again, and Mike bristled with guns.

Eddie half-expected the lamia to break him in two, but she didn't resist at all. She raised her head to meet Eddie's gaze as Jim set him carefully on his feet, nodded once and relaxed her neck again.

"Mierda," Mike muttered.

Eddie crawled into the embrace of the lamia. Her flesh was warm and she smelled as much of woman as she did of snake. Her torso, certainly, was all woman, dusky and voluptuous. If he hadn't felt on death's door, Eddie might have been excited to be this close to a beautiful woman. The danger, the fear that any moment she might rise up and smash him flat, only added to the thrill of the moment. Shaking like a bad drunk with the DTs, he curled into her arms, attached himself like an infant, and drank.

The blood that poured from her many wounds and trickled onto Eddie was as hot as his own. The snake heads of Miriam's hair hissed at him gently. It sounded like voices shushing a baby. Eddie listened to their voices and almost slipped into oblivion.

But then he felt the burning and the weariness and the trembling of his limbs fall away. He didn't feel refreshed or rejuvenated—he felt exhausted and beat up, but the effects of the venom were gone. He didn't feel like he was on the brink of dying anymore.

He dug into his pocket for the cup. It felt strangely intimate and invasive to lie beside the lamia and milk her, but it would have felt even more wrong to kneel and treat her like an animal. She had made terrible decisions, but she had paid for them, and in the end, she was as much a person as Eddie was. Eddie's heart roiled with all sorts of feelings, and he found to his surprise that one of the strongest was gratitude. As respectfully as he could, he filled the bottom of the jacks cup with the warm bluish milk of the lamia Miriam. When he had what he thought was probably enough, he put the cap back on the cup and stood.

He met her gaze one last time through lidded eyes.

"I forgot," she hissed simply.

Eddie nodded solemnly. "I know," he said. "I won't forget."

Then her last breath rattled in her throat and the lamia was gone. Eddie didn't feel bad for her—she'd killed way too many people, and done worse, to arouse his compassion. But he didn't hate her. In the end, he didn't even really find her monstrous.

He took a deep breath and stepped back. When he was sure he could face the others without tears in his eyes, he surveyed the damage.

It was total. There were bodies all over the room, snake, lizard, and human, and mutant combinations of all stripes. Eddie saw mongoose corpses, too—none of the preacher's furry allies had survived. The dog was smashed to pieces, the headless priest bled out, the preacher smashed into sanctified marmalade, the totem poles knocked over. The Nehushtan was either pulverized or hidden in the wreckage. Still, there was something about the room that nagged at his perception, something positive, something that made him feel almost happy.

Mike handed him his guns. Eddie checked to see that both weapons were loaded, snapped the Glock into its holster and reattached the Remington 870 to its shoulder strap while he thought about what it could be. It felt good to be armed again.

On the other hand, the junk in his pockets had been surprisingly useful.

"You okay?" Mike asked.

Eddie snorted and cut away the tourniquet with his pocketknife. "All things considered," he said, "not too bad."

Then it hit him.

The legs were gone.

He looked up and saw an ordinary concrete ceiling, undergirded with pipes and fluorescent lights, spattered with blood, but with no sign of the field of ice and the dangling legs of the damned that had previously haunted his vision.

Eddie took a deep breath and let it out slowly. "Yeah," he said. "I feel good."

Twitch looked around at the mess. "No amount of bleach is going to clean this up," the fairy chuckled.

Jim shook his head and bent to pick up the charcoal grill of smoldering incense coals by its struts. Eddie watched as the singer walked slowly around the carnage, shaking coals out onto fallen totem poles and into puddles of cleaning fluids, throwing the last of them indiscriminately into the janitorial closet. By the time he was done, the basement was on fire.

Eddie started towards the stairs. In front of him a rusty iron chain ground slowly from right to left at his chest level. Severed human arms, legs and heads hung pinned to the chain like so much laundry on a clothesline. The mouths of the severed heads opened and closed and their eyes bulged in Eddie's direction like they were calling to him.

Eddie shook his head and walked right through the chain. He ached and he was exhausted, but he was alive and free.

Did that mean, he wondered, that his vision of death in a burning palace was a true one?

Or had he been inspired to fight on by a false vision, thereby making the vision true? Or at least, preserving the possibility of its truth?

He shook the thoughts out of his head as he crossed the ground floor towards the glass doors. Really, he knew, he wouldn't know the answer to anything until it was all over.

"I hope Adrian made it," Mike muttered.

Eddie checked his watch. "We still got fifteen minutes," he said. "We'll get there in time. How are your fingers?"

"Fingers?" Mike opened and closed his hands experimentally. "Fine. Why?"

"We got a gig," Eddie reminded him. "Unless you got cash you ain't told me about, we gotta play or we don't have enough money to get out of Oklahoma."

"*Cagado.*"

"That's about the size of it," Eddie agreed. He pushed open the doors and he and Mike walked out into the cooling air of the early evening.

ABOUT THE AUTHOR

D.J. Butler (Dave) is a novelist living in the Rocky Mountain northwest. His training is in law, and he worked as a securities lawyer at a major international firm and inhouse at two multinational semiconductor manufacturers before taking up writing fiction. He is a lover of language and languages, a guitarist and self-recorder, and a serious reader. He is married to a powerful and clever woman and together they have three devious children.

Dave writes fantasy, science fiction, space opera, steampunk, cyberpunk, superhero, alternate history, dystopian fiction, horror and related genres for all audiences. His novels *Crecheling* and *City of the Saints* are available from WordFire Press, and his middle reader steampunk adventure series, The Extraordinary Journeys of Clockwork Charlie, launches soon with the novel *The Kidnap Plot* (Knopf, 2016).

Read about all of Dave's fiction projects at:

http://davidjohnbutler.com.

OTHER WORDFIRE PRESS TITLES BY D.J. BUTLER

Rock Band Fights Evil:

Hellhound On My Trail

Crow Jane

Devil Sent the Rain

Crecheling

Our list of other WordFire Press authors and titles is always growing.
To find out more and to see our selection of titles, visit us at:

wordfirepress.com

www.ingramcontent.com/pod-product-compliance
Lightning Source LLC
Chambersburg PA
CBHW020530120726
47904CB00003B/1029